ISBN 13: 978-1-84481-028-4

ISBN 10: 1-84481-028-3

AF256980

The Run

D. Amer

Now

There comes a moment in a man's life when everything that was before has to balance with everything that is yet to come. Some people call this Karma, others will tell you it's a form of Zen. For me it is simply Now.

Of course, intellectually and even philosophically elegant as that may sound, there are some details which once taken into account will make you change your mind.

Like the fact that I'm on my knees, with my hands behind my head, staring at the shadowy form of a man holding a snub nosed .38 and pointing it directly at the forehead of Alex Logan Esquire, a.k.a. yours truly, from no less than a foot away.

It's not a great situation to be in, especially when you're negotiating which is, actually, exactly what I was doing at that moment in time. Granted, it's difficult to see the leverage I possessed but that will become evident in a moment, along with the curious journey that took to that seminal moment in my life where, like Schrodinger's famous cat I was in stasis: neither dead nor alive until the finger that was pressing on the trigger of the gun, reached the 10lbs of pressure required to trip the hammer and fire a 125 grain bullet at a speed of upwards of 770 feet per second, directly into my brain.

I know that this is not quite what Schrodinger envisioned as the collapse of his probability wave but I am willing to wager that it's a pretty cool way to visualize his, admittedly difficult to understand, thought experiment.

The .30 Special pointing at my forehead, in this particular case, is the measuring device that will determine whether I am dead or alive. Its moment of measurement represented by the pull of a trigger and the fall of a hammer on a primer embedded in a metal cased cartridge. Kneeling there, hands behind my head, forehead an easy target, I am visualizing the entire process in a deconstructionist way that strips back the layers of time and creates, for me, the perfect way to relieve the pressure of the moment and think clearly.

I know you think that is odd. Let me assure you this won't be the first time you will think this though, quite possibly, there is a more than slim possibility that it will be the last.

Bear with me.

The man's face is a mystery to me. Hidden by the shadows cast by the powerful lights behind him. I know his name: Ned. Though that may be a decoy.

At times like this a respectable, law-abiding citizen has several options. Option One: give up. Give the man with the gun exactly what he wants. It may work or it may not, but you can understand why most people don't take the time to factor in the possibilities. Presented with a gun with a barrel pointed directly at you, they tend to fold. Do as the man with the gun says and hope for the best.

I don't fall within the normal distribution of your statistical Bell Curve. I am a little perverse that way.

Option Two: Plead for clemency and hope for mercy. It takes little insight to realize that the chances of your average respectable, law-abiding citizen finding themselves at the docs, past midnight, on their knees, with a gun pointed at their heads are pretty slim. This means that I am neither respectable nor law-abiding, though both of these characterizations are up for debate.

Seeing how both respectability and obedience to the laws that run a particular society are a matter of perception and interpretation the correct answer to either question relies on interpretation. To my eyes I am both respectable and, within context, law-abiding. But that is a purely semantic approach that takes into account the network effect of linked behaviors.

I am sure the man with the gun will disagree which is what makes this situation particularly sticky. Depending on interpretation he may be, even when his current action is taken into account, more law-abiding than I.

Which leads me to Option Three: Determine the weight of the factors that lead to the trigger being pulled and the gun being fired against the weight of the factors that call for the exact opposite.

This is not so hard to imagine. Consider that if I (or you) happened to be Schrodinger's cat, in order to survive we would have to arrest the collapse of the probability wave and remain in stasis forever. Neither dead, nor alive is much more preferable to being definitely dead. Avoiding the certainty of the first of the probabilities increases the likelihood of returning to the warm embrace of the second.

All we'd have to do, in our virtual cat state, to achieve that option is find a plausible way to influence the willingness of the person with the measuring apparatus to carry out the measurement.

You see what I've done here. I know the man with the gun wants, somewhere deep in him, to press the trigger and erase the narrative of my existence forever. But he is not operating in a vacuum. His presence here has been dictated by other forces and other events which, when linked correctly, weave a web of interactions and connections that lead to a degree of accountability.

His actions, in other words, are not free of consequences.

A smart cat, like you and I, just needs a means of bringing those consequences to the present so that they can command his attention and stay the increasing pressure being applied by his finger on the trigger.

And we'd have to do this quickly enough. With sufficient aplomb to avoid triggering the idea that what we have here is a modified version of Option Two which is most likely to trigger him (pun unintended).

It's a predicament. Especially when Option One, which is what he really wants us to go for before he pulls that trigger, is never really on the cards. Never will be.

Tricky.

I have your attention now. Understanding what we, virtual cats, would have to do in order to stay alive is only half the battle. I understand.

The real question is how.

To answer that however we now need to go back in time together. To the crazy moment when all this started.

1 – Data World

Everything is data. The moment you understand that you have a key to a puzzle that no one wants you to understand. Not the government. Not the corporations. Not your boss. Not even your crazy ex-wife who left you for a man she hardly knew because he made her feel alive, she said; whatever that means.

Your crazy ex-wife may not actually know or even understand any of this. Of course, when I say "your" I mean "mine" I am deflecting here, of course, because it's difficult to admit that I was dumped by the person I thought I loved and she broke my heart.

Whatever. Data. That's what we need to talk about of course. It's everywhere. It's in the things you purchase and the things you don't. It's in your viewing habits. The places you frequent. The people you talk to. The political parties you join. The government services you attend.

Data is what keeps the world spinning because everyone collects it and everyone wants it. These two sets of "everyone" are not always compatible with each other and in some cases they may not even overlap.

Ah, I know you're dying to understand what I am saying. Consider this: data is the cheapest commodity on the planet. Don't listen to those who say data is expensive. It actually is not. But just like crude oil or industrial or unprocessed diamonds data on its own is not really worth more than dirt and now that I think of it dirt may actually be more expensive at that point.

But just like crude oil and unprocessed diamonds data, once processed, is actually worth a lot. A heck of a lot.

Processing defines it the same way processing of crude oil and unprocessed diamonds refines them and gives them value.

The value of processed data lies in the context of the reality it reveals.

Think of it this way, and I will for the sake of my example allow things to get a little personal. The massive amounts of data captured by face recognition cameras may constitute a breach of privacy and maybe personal freedom but they don't actually signify anything; anything at all, until they are processed.

Who cares if you have a million faces on camera that have been captured visiting Manhattan Mall on 33rd Street and Sixth Avenue until out of those one million faces you pick up the one you know and have been looking for who can then be seen visiting not Manhattan Mall but a particular room at Hotel Pennsylvania on 100 West 33rd Street.

Twice a week. Wednesdays and Fridays.

That particular piece of data now begins to acquire context but it's not yet quite real. Reality arises when another piece of data places a particular seller of dodgy financial products in the same hotel, on the same floor, in the same room on the same days.

These data points, tracked, acquire context and intent. Their purpose then is revealed simply through their movements in the world of data. Their story, revealed, also impacts mine.

That is how processed data works. Seemingly meaningless, small and irrelevant data points, once linked, acquire meaning that reveals what they are actually doing and, even more important, what they're going to do.

To a data guy like myself processed data is gold. Armed with it I can do a lot of things. I can, for instance, arrange for Swatting to take place by placing some of the attributes of these two data points to pop up in law enforcement databases.

The great systems that surround us then. The ones that we entrust to safeguard the sanctity of our everyday, kick into gear and do their thing.

Hotels in the middle of Manhattan are raided. News teams are alerted. Data points find themselves being busted in by masked, armed men in the middle of a midday tryst.

Oh, I am being chivalrous here because I don't really want to contemplate the cruder, underlying reality of their act. Not just yet. But I am sure you get the point and understand the importance of data.

Which leads things to me. Alex Logan Esquire, well, not quite a lawyer any more. I gave that up years ago when practicing law in New York became a game of swimming in a pool full of sharks who appeared to have bigger teeth than me and sharper senses.

But they didn't understand data. Or rather they understood it OK. They understood the value of its existence and the power of its kept secrets. They just didn't understand how to make sure those secrets were kept.

That's what I do. I am the keeper of secrets. For real. I needed a job after I gave up practicing law. I knew all the big firms in the city. I knew what their needs were. Which is why I set up the one and only personal data crypt. Alex Logan, for a fee, will take all your secrets. Encrypt them using the world's only unbreakable cipher and hand deliver them to whoever they are intended for. All, for a hefty fee.

I know what you're thinking. Risky job. What's the pay? Is it truly as secure as advertised?

Let me put your mind to instant rest. Yes, it's exactly as advertised.

In theory, any type of encryption can be broken given enough time, energy and processing power. Our current encryption methods are secure because they require impractical amounts of at least one of those three factors.

That's not a stable situation however. An interested party with sufficient motivation and resources can actually throw enough computing power at it to break pretty much anything.

State-sponsored actors have deep pockets and very focused minds. In my time as a data runner, yep; that's what I am, I have crossed the paths of Russians and Uruguayans, Argentinians and British, Germans and French, Israeli and Americans. Yep, I am that good and the job is that crazy.

But it pays well.

That's what got me in trouble. Or really, it contributed. It was my ex that really got me into trouble. Or rather her lover. The peddler of dodgy financial products that really should come with a government wealth warning attached.

Something along the lines of: "Investing in these shares is like putting all your money on fire".

But it wasn't my ex I was thinking that day when Slater came to see me.

I knew Slater from way back when I still used to practice law. Good guy, most times. A little bit of a hustler at times, particularly when it came to milking big buck clients. Slater knew exactly what to say and when to say it to maximize the value of any contract for himself and his firm.

A darling. But with me he was always alright. Until that day.

"Hey Alex, you're still up for one more job?" That was how he started. It was in the middle of the day. I was at home. I work from home. Another thing Wendy held against me.

"Real men have an office," she yelled at me once during a heated moment between us. Like it's the real estate that defines the masculinity of its occupants.

Well, I did not have an office. You know the cost of office space in Manhattan? Besides office space introduces some job-specific vulnerabilities which, in my case, I found intolerable. It is the space where someone can reach you during 'office hours only' and there isn't such a thing where I am concerned.

It is the space where you keep … what? Files of clients? The secrets you're entrusted with which you can never divulge?

Lists of … I struggled to come up with any valid reason why I would ever need an office.

I work in very specific ways. People give me data. The kind of data they do not want others to see. And if they happen to see it they will never understand it.

That means encryption. Not just good encryption or pretty good encryption. Unbreakable encryption. Really unbreakable.

"Just how good is that encryption of yours?" When Slater asked me that question I knew it wasn't an academic one. He was testing me. Testing the algorithm I was using.

If you're even remotely online and a tiny bit of a data rat you know that encryption is a bugbear. On the web it slows down traffic to a crawl which is why its use is a trade-off. A little bit of security for a little bit of loss of speed. No one however, I repeat, no one, wants to see web traffic slowdown to dial-up modem bit rates.

So no one really uses RSA. The Rivest-Shamir-Adleman encryption algorithm is one of the most powerful forms of encryption in the world. It supports incredibly key lengths, and it is typical to see 2048- and 4096- bit keys.

RSA is an asymmetric encryption algorithm. This means that there are two separate encryption keys. One encrypts information and is public for everyone to see. The other can decrypt that data and is private.

Because RSA slows everything down on the web it's used to encrypt another, faster algorithm that is symmetric and much, much faster. It's a little like having keyless entry to your car but disguising the fob into the shape of a lighter.

Don't fall asleep yet. There is more. There is, for instance, the Advanced Encryption Standard, commonly known as AES. This is usually paired with RSA as its symmetric partner. AES is so strong that it has become the official encryption standard of the US government.

Then there is Quantum cryptography. This is a very powerful computing method that uses the uncertainty inherent to the quantum realm to perform tasks. The computers we use on a day-to-day basis are binary. That means they use the numbers one and zero to compute. In other words, the bits of data used to perform computations can only be in one of two states.

Quantum bits, or "qubits" can be in both states at once. Which means a quantum computer that's working on a problem can be in all possible states at once. Schrodinger's cat situation again and the collapse of the probability wave.

Then there's photonic encryption. Traditional computers use electrons to whiz about the CPU's pathways and actually drive the computations of the machine. While electrons are incredibly fast, photons are much faster. In fact, since photons are the fundamental component of light, they go as fast as is possible in this universe. At least as far as we know.

This is why photonic computers are such an exciting idea. However, there's a mountain of practical problems that have to be solved before we can have any hope of a photonic computer that can compete with general purpose silicon CPUs.

The same goes for DNA cryptography. DNA, is the most ancient information carrying code that we know of. Every living creature on Earth has their entire evolutionary history locked away inside their cells. DNA computers are an emerging form of radical computing that, like quantum computing, promises to break existing strong encryption as a triviality. Unlike quantum computing, DNA computing is very slow.

I know of at least two world governments who are active on these fronts, throwing insane amounts of money to make sure that their secrets stay secret and they can break into and uncover the secrets of others.

That is the great irony of our time. Just like being infidelity, unbreakable encryption is seen as a trait you deem desirable for your situation but totally do not want to see others practice.

So Slater was right to challenge me. After all he was about to wire 20Gs into my account and deliver as much again at completion.

I never said I was cheap. Nor did I say I couldn't afford to pay the rent of an office. It's just that an office had nothing to offer me more than my place in The Bronx.

I live in Mt Eden. At 1700 Grand Concourse at the Capri. It's a twelve story building with a 24-hour doorman and it was the place Wendy and I called home. When there was a Wendy and I.

When she left she took the flat screen TV and the couch and I never replaced them. The one-bedroom flat on the twelfth floor we'd shared for five years suddenly appeared roomier. Quieter.

I stayed and worked.

Slater was standing still on the other side of my desk. He was expecting an answer and the question was a test.

"Give me a document," I said. "Anything, something verifiable quickly," he looked at me a little puzzled. "I want you to be able to verify fidelity. Encryption, really good encryption is not just about making something inaccessible. A good hammer and some excellently placed overhead swings will do that for you. You need to also be able to access the information once it arrives where it should,"

"Ah. I see," he said. He gave me a USB stick. A small, metal thumb drive, elegantly designed to be paired down to the slimmest possible profile. All rounded edges and a capped end. It was, I guessed, about the size of a lozenge. Mainly because in case of being discovered one would have to ingest it.

"What's on here?" I asked him.

"My driving license and passport numbers,"

"Ok." I took the thumb drive from him and inserted it in my laptop. I've always expected this kind of challenge and was fully prepared for it.

While I talked to Slater my laptop ran a diagnostic, checked the thumb drive for viruses. Trojans. Anything suspect disguised as malware.

It was actually clean which surprised me a little. I would have expected someone like Slater to try something a little edgier. Then again, since Wendy's departure I'd come to consider human nature as naturally predisposed to bad behavior.

"This won't take long," I said and pressed enter.

I'd configured my laptop especially expecting just this kind of request.

Not every form of encryption is the same.

Theory will only get you so far. When you need fast, reliable, unbreakable encryption you have to have a fact-based approach that works. Every time.

Of all the methods of encryption ever devised, only one has been mathematically proved to be completely secure. It is called the Vernam cipher or one-time pad. The worth of all other ciphers is based on computational security. If a cipher is computationally secure this means the probability of cracking the encryption key using current computational technology and algorithms within a reasonable time is supposedly extremely small, yet not impossible.

Given sufficient funds and motivation the amount of computer time and raw computational power required is never a sufficient deterrent.

In my business motivation is never in short supply. This means that all the other ingredients necessary to crack a supposedly unbreakable cipher are in plentiful supply. That's why nothing gets transmitted through the networks. Nothing is stored in the cloud. Nothing is encrypted in any other way than what I can provide.

In theory, every cryptographic algorithm except for the Vernam cipher can be broken given enough ciphertext and time.

For example the public key cryptosystems such as PGP and RSA are based on the following: Calculate an integer N such that it has only two prime number factors f1 and f2. This triad of integers forms the basis of the encryption and decryption keys used in PK cryptosystems. The security of these systems is simply based on the computational difficulty of calculating f2 and f1 from N if N is a very large integer. To break this cipher N must be factored, and at the time these systems were devised the best publicly available factoring algorithms would take millions of years to factor a 200 digit number. This does not logically exclude the possibility of a new factoring algorithm being discovered, or the existence of a secret factoring algorithm, or the invention of technology capable of running current factoring algorithms at high speed.

Forgive me if I am boring you with necessary details. The very fact you need guys like me is because people like you get bored with these details.

Your secrets never stay secret for very long. Your secure cloud storage is never secure. Your encryption algorithms always fail to protect you.

In 1917 during the First World War the American scientist Gilbert Vernam was given the task of inventing an encryption method the Germans could not break by AT&T. What was devised was the only provably unbreakable encryption scheme known to this day. Compared with most cryptosystems it is very simple. To use a one-time pad, you need 2 copies of the "pad" (also known as the key) which is a block of truly random data at least as long as the message you wish to encode. If the data on the pad is not truly random, the security of the pad is compromised.

One-time pads are used in pairs. The more copies of a given pad, the greater the likelihood is that one may be captured, in which case the message encrypted by the pad will be compromised. One copy of the pad is kept by each user, and pads must be exchanged via a secure channel (e.g. face to face on disks or USB keys). Pads must only be used once.

The fastest method of encrypting and decrypting a message with a one-time pad is with a computer. If you do choose this method keep the pad on a USB key, CD or DVD and destroy it completely once used. Supposedly deleted data can be retrieved and reconstructed from storage media, so never store pads on your hard drive or keep the medium holding the pad one it has been used. The message recipient should apply the same precautions. Using a networked computer for implementing the encryption/decryption should be avoided because of possible eavesdropping.

A computer simplifies the process because the message and pad are encoded in binary. Each character is represented internally by a computer as a unique combination of zeros and ones called bits, for example the letter 'b' is composed of the eight bits '1100010'. This binary number is 98 in decimal. To encrypt the message each bit of each letter in the plaintext is combined with the corresponding letters' bit in the pad in sequence using a transformation called the bitwise exclusive or (abbreviated to XOR).

I take one more precaution. I use only one pad. Deliver the message in person. Deliver the key upon payment.

Risky?

Maybe. There are those who'd consider killing the messenger as the best means of ensuring a secret stays secret. But they don't know if this messenger has a failsafe. A dead man's switch to be activated on demise.

Slater, of course, didn't know any of this. He was only interested in testing my encryption.

I quickly pulled up the files. Encrypted them. Erased the originals on purpose. Passed the flash drive back to him.

"Here. All done."

He took it from me. "Already?"

"Yeah, it's quick."

"We shall see how good it is now," he said. He was already busy fitting the flash drive to his phone. My guess is he was transmitting it, someone, somewhere had set up a Cray, maybe. Something fancier? They'd try and crack it using the original files as reference.

Knowing what was already encrypted gave you an instant advantage. But not in this case. Not with the Vernam Cipher.

"Come back when you want a job done," I said.

Slater looked surprised. He probably had expected to get a call already so he could surprise me. He hesitated a little longer, shuffled his weight from one foot to the other. Looked at his phone.

The device remained silent.

Slater shuffled some more. The silence between us was getting awkward. He said at last: "OK, I will be back."

I watched him go thinking that for the prices he'd already agreed with me this was a job that required the utmost discretion. Encryption was only part of what was needed here.

I didn't know it at the time but time wasn't something I had plenty of. Ignorance is a form of protection. The human brain simply can't handle knowing the future.

"Take your time," I said. I watched him walk out the room and heard the door slam shut behind him, as he left.

2 – The Job

"What you gave me is bullshit!" Slater was clearly not happy with something. He was back in my living room. He wasn't alone. This time he'd come with two goons who pushed in the moment I opened my door. Armpits bulging with concealed guns and tailored black suits straining as they moved.

"Hard to crack, right?" I quipped and watched him go very still which was his habit when he didn't quite know how to handle something.

"Bullshit!" he repeated a little less forcefully.

"You tried to crack it?" He nodded that he had. "Threw everything at it that you could think of?" He nodded again. "The goons here for insurance, am I right? In case I really tricked you?" he shrugged that one. The muscle closest to me let out a slight hiss. He didn't like my characterization. Tough.

I knew they weren't his. Most probably whoever had hired him had supplied them and bankrolled the computers that had tried to break what couldn't be broken.

"How does it work?" he asked.

"I can't tell you that. If I did, like the Coca Cola company, I would be out of business. It's my trade secret."

"No. I mean how does this work? You encrypt it and then?"

"I deliver it, decrypt it. The client gets it."

"No way. That means you see what's there."

"I couldn't give a tosh of what you're trying to hide," I said.

"My client would need the key,"

"Then my cipher might be compromised. So, sorry. No key. I decrypt it, get paid. Walk."

"Decrypt it then." He gave me back the thumb drive.

I took it from him, made to insert it in my laptop.

"Not there," he stopped me. "How do I know you haven't stored the files already?"

Fair point, I conceded. He didn't. "Where then?" I asked.

"Here, in this." Slater motioned to one of the goons. The one nearest the door. He had a laptop bag slung over one shoulder. He unslung it. Reached inside. Took out a small laptop. Gave it to Slater. Slater gave it to me.

I took it.

It was a small networked unit. Already on. I guessed that whoever had hired Slater was monitoring the device, probably logging keystrokes. Certainly mirroring the screen.

I put the laptop on my desk. Turned it so that Slater and the goons could see exactly what I was doing. My back now to them. I killed the connection to the web. "Sorry, no peeking," I said.

I inserted the thumb drive Slater had given me. Took out another one from a pocket. "The key," I said. Inserted it. It took me three seconds to bring up the decrypted files on screen. "Satisfied?"

Slater looked at them. "How?"

"That's what you're paying me all that money for," I said. Watched him nod to himself. I turned to the laptop and pulled out my thumb drive. I placed it carefully on the desk and reaching around behind it, I pulled out a small, silver-colored, black handled hammer.

I swung once, twice, three times, hitting the drive hard each time. Watched it break up in tiny pieces. The ends badly flattened, the inside smashed completely.

"Security," I said. "No key. No secrets. I do that every time."

Slater nodded to himself again.

There is a predictability to behavior. Patterns that are repeated because the acceptable boundaries allow only so many choices. People will, invariably, take one of the choices available to them.

You'd think someone who knows this and understands it would have been smart enough to see that his own wife was cheating on him, but we all have our blind spots. Wendy was mine.

I reached out and re-enabled the network option on the laptop. Gave whoever was mirroring the screen a clear look at what I'd decrypted. Probably me too. The camera light was off but that didn't mean anything.

"Happy?" I asked.

Slater's phone rang on cue. He answered. Listened for a moment. Nodded to himself. Turned it off. "OK," he said at last. "You've got yourself a deal," he put his hand out in a handshake and I reached out and took it.

I only have two rules: Rule number one, I get to see the data I encrypt. It's a tough one, but shit; it's my life, my reputation, my job. If someone doesn't like it they don't have to come to me.

It works. To date, I have never had to turn a client away because I saw something so unsavory that it left me with no option but to say "no'.

Rule number two: I need to know who the client is.

I know some data running outfits, big firms, lots of people. They will work with chains of contact two and three layers deep. Talk through lawyers representing trusts that represent offshore companies.

Your own grandmother could be hiring you to do a job and you'd never even know. Me. I need to know.

Why? That's my personal protection filter. Clients unhappy to show their face or their data are the kind of clients I don't want anyway.

Slater, of course, knows my rules.

"Well?" I asked him. He shuffled from foot to foot.

"Alex," he began, I knew what he was going to say. I let him say it anyway. "Any way we can bend the rules a little on this one? Maybe up the price? Double it?"

It was never gonna happen. Eighty thousand might sound a lot for a day's work but it's not when you're in hospital or worse. My rules are designed to protect me. And they work.

"You know the answer to that one," I told Slater. "Take the goons and walk."

"Alex, wait."

"You're wasting my time."

"Goddamn it!" Slater lost his cool a little.

I sat still waiting him out. He would either walk or work and I would get my 40K. At that time of the day though, the only thing I could think of was that I was really, really hungry and I should order some pizza.

Something with pepperoni and double cheese. Wendy loved double cheese. The thought of her made me shut down. I was suddenly icy cold and willing Slater and co to simply walk out.

"Alex, I am sorry – I," he began. Then his phone rang.

It confirmed for me that the camera on the laptop was on despite the light not showing. So they had put in a keylogger, of that I was pretty sure, hoping to catch my algorithm working.

Not smart. Predictable.

That was good. Predictable is trustworthy. I tried explaining this to Liz, one door down.

"Trust is an algorithm," I explained.

"Alex you trust no one," she laughed that broad laugh of hers, trying to distract me from the subtext of the moment. I stopped trusting people when Wendy walked.

"Not true," I smiled back. The smile didn't quite reach my eyes but she didn't seem to notice. "Trust is a calculation. A prediction. It's what we feel when we know how someone will react to a specific stimulus in a specific moment in time."

"Com'on!" she shrugged, her laugh contagious.

"No, really."

"Tell me,"

"You, for instance," I said and watched her become a little more serious. She always did that when I talked about her like that and I never quite knew what she was thinking. I did know however that she paid attention when I did.

Wendy left a hole in my life. No. She tore a hole through my soul. Stopped me from wanting anything. Stopped me from living.

Liz and Sam were the only real friends I had left after the breakup. Everyone else had either blamed me or taken Wendy's side or felt too awkward to interact. They'd all drifted away.

"Ok. Looks like we have a deal," Slater said. Just like that. I knew he'd agree; or at least his client would agree.

I sit there quietly, thinking about nothing in particular. Just before a job, I always find it best to rest my mind, focus on nothing. A kind of personal prep, if you like.

The two goons are at strategic points in the room. One stands by the door, guarding the way in and, I suppose, making sure I stay put, though I choose not to see it that way.

The other stands behind by the window, looking at the street outside.

"They're here," he says at last and I feel the tension in the room rise a couple of notches. The goon by the door stands taller, as if that were ever possible, his large frame stiff.

Slater nods to himself and I can't help but notice that he also appears tense. This should be good.

"Alex please behave," Slater whispers to me and I nod though, to be fair, I always behave. I mean everything is really behavior and I behave as in deliver what I think is necessary for me to deliver through my conduct. I am not on this planet to please anyone anymore.

Not quite true, I think. But true enough. At least for now.

I can hear the vague screech of tires and the telling noise of heavy car doors being slammed. The silence. Then in the corridor outside my door, feet.

Then: A heavy knock on the door.

Goon by the door opens it.

Another goon, virtually identical is standing outside. Explains the heavy knock.

Ok, I tell myself. This is a goon show. The thought makes me smile but I catch it in time and my lips curl in a barely perceptible smirk.

Slater notices. "Alex!" he hisses. I nod again. Try hard to keep a straight face as the client enters with a practiced theatricality that tells me that the whole goon show is more for his benefit than mine. He expects it because, you know, big cheese entitlement and all that.

Sometimes I think Liz is right. The more things change, the more they remain the same.

I stayed seated, analyzing the figure that walked through the door and made its way towards me. Slick black suit. Tailored. Very expensive. Black Italian leather shoes. Shiny enough to reflect the room, I thought when I first saw them. White shirt. Red tie. Manicured hands. I dragged my eyes to his face. He looked vaguely familiar. Then it clicked. OK.

"You know who I am?" That was his introduction to me. Dickhead! I didn't or rather I never thought much about who he might have been and when I saw him my brain had to piece it all together from news reports and the occasional article in the sleazier websites. Now it all made more sense to me.

"Kind of," I said and caught Slater's imploring eyes. "I mean I do, of course. Just not the capacity you're here, in," I corrected quickly. I tried to sound suitably surprised.

The dickhead standing before me with an air of unwarranted self-importance was the oldest child of the man in the Oval Office. That would make the goons around me Secret Service, I thought. And it would make little ol' Alex, data runner extraordinaire, a paid stooge of the U.S. government.

What did Slater have to do with all this?

"I am here as a private citizen," he said. He had a smooth, polished voice oozing confidence. His whole demeanor was one of condescension, as if he was doing me a favor being here.

I hadn't yet agreed to take the job.

"Swell place," he looked around with the genuine interest of a visitor to a museum where specimens of dinosaurs are on display. "Quaint," he beamed and I wanted to punch him.

While the POTUS was in office his son was painting Washington red by some reports. From nightclub romps in the VIP suite to all-night parties that no one would afterwards ever admit to.

A man's life is his own. And what he wants to do with his penis is his business. I really couldn't care less about any of it. But POTUS Jr. was a hunter. He fancied himself a Hemingway, styled his hair and beard after the man. Never missed an opportunity to be photographed with a harpooned big fish or a freshly killed big game.

What's the big deal? You'd ask. Hunters hunt. Many hunters are also conservationists, passionate advocates of controlled animal populations and vociferous activists for the establishment of special protection zones.

True. POTUS Jr. wasn't one of those. As a matter of fact, a normal human being would be hard-pressed to understand just what POTUS Jr. really was. He self-styled himself as a playboy though everyone knew it was daddy's money that was bankrolling the lifestyle, and he often said he was an angel investor, the man who made the "next big thing, possible."

Some human beings just rub you the wrong way. POTUS Jr. had that talent. No one liked him.

"You're the man who can get the job done," he was speaking again. He hated silences. Apparently. Liked to fill the air with words.

"What job is that?" I asked quietly and sensed more than saw Slater stiffen beside me.

"Well, you know. The package," he laughed again. Looked at the Secret Service goons around him for confirmation of the value of his half-joke. No one said anything.

Like, I said. No one liked him.

"Well," he continued unperturbed. "I have some information that I would like you to deliver to someone. And for that information I will pay you a lot of money," he spoke slowly, enunciating every word, like he was speaking to a child.

"Half now – " I cut him off.

"What?"

"Half now. Pay half now. Right now. As a retainer. Otherwise, no go."

He frowned. "Ah, I see." I wasn't sure what he thought he saw but I waited.

"We have the funds in the holding account ready to be transferred," said Slater, talking directly to POTUS Jr.

"Ah, right. Thank you. Thank you." He said to Slater, "See?" he turned to me. "All handled. We are good to go. How do we do this then?"

Like I said I don't always take the job. When I do I try to pick it. I need the money like everyone else. I also need to be able to sleep at night without worrying whether I'd wake up in the morning.

I take time to vet my clients and I take time to check the data I deliver. Unusual and yeah, a little invasive. Then again we live in interesting times.

The dickhead's presence here had blindsided me. I am not used to celebrity clients. The ones who usually need my service have secrets they want to hide: financial data. The odd double-dealing. Some invention. The reason I check is that the moment I see anything that's likely to get me killed I back off.

The mob's tried to recruit me a couple of times. They thoughts if they had me run all their comms no one would be able to eavesdrop. They don't get encryption I guess. And they didn't quite understand what I offered.

A couple of Wall Street types in the past had me run their tips. Insider trading, done right, can deliver a lot of cash. Those I did. I am not here to police people's ethics.

No one tries to hire me too often. I am not cheap. I see their secrets and know who they are. It makes for an unusual, volatile situation. At least in their minds. Eventually they back off.

Now this.

"Alex, the number," Slater said to me trying to sound really professional. I could see he was tense. I hesitated for a moment weighing the consequences of just saying no. I'm no idiot. The dickhead was here. The Secret Service were here. Slater was here. Everyone had come to see me. They could, I suppose, all go back where they'd come from but it was unlikely to go smoothly and the U.S. Government is harder to scare off, especially when it's personal and I had the sense that a refusal from me was likely to make it so.

I hate being boxed in.

"Are you going to give me the number?" Slater repeated. He was looking at me intently like he was trying to say something. The Dickhead was looking around like he was at some Safari Park. The Secret Service goons might as well be carved from stone for all the reaction they were showing.

"Sure," I said and slater relaxed. I reeled off a twelve digit number. The Caymans are a British protectorate. The U.S. has no business there. "$20K," I added, almost as an afterthought.

I was using the space to think. The Dickhead, I noticed had some cologne on. A kind of undertoned lemon-based scent. It added to my sense of unease and, at the same time, pissed me off.

Neuroscientists will tell you that anger is reactive aggression. Individuals who show impairment in the ability to alter behavioral responding when actions no longer receive their expected rewards should be (and are in the context of psychopathy) associated with increased anger.

Anger overturns the feeling of victimization that occurs when a situation is spinning out of control and we no longer receive the expected reward, and transforms the victim into aggressor.

It also impairs judgement.

Slater was as good as his word. I watched on my phone as the balance in my Cayman island account updated in real time. You've got to love technology. I had just made $20K. All I had was to deliver some information.

"We're good?" Slater asked. Funny thing doing what I do. You begin to notice the little things. Because I am dealing with secrets and my fee is always a lot of cash I notice the way people react after they've paid me or right after they've handed over secrets they'd rather no one knew about.

Some responses are cinematic. Others are questions delivered in a higher-than-usual pitch. A sure sign of stressors being felt. A few are practically belligerent. Their suppressed aggression a defense mechanism designed to make them feel they are back in control.

The Secret Service goons were still cast of stone. Their roles in this drama completely rigid and defined by their job. We are all actors on a stage in some sense. We move constantly from a state of relative dissatisfaction to one of less dissatisfaction.

In case you think that's the amoeba response to adverse stimulus you'd be right. We're just slightly higher-order animals, but only slightly. I was pissed that I'd boxed myself in a corner. The only way out of it was to take the damn job, deliver the information, collect the rest of my money and be on my merry way.

Slater was pissed because I was making him look bad in front of his boss. He sold himself as a guy who calls the shots and provides specific solutions to specific problems. Was the Dickhead dissatisfied with something, somehow? Hard to tell.

But he was here, standing in front of me, in my Bronx living room that I used to share with Wendy so it was certain that he was in no Zen state of happiness.

The Secret Service goons? They too, right at that moment, must have been feeling dissatisfaction. Their entire existence was one of mobility, getting into and out of higher-risk and lower-risk situations.

Which one was I right now? Hard to tell from where I was sat. "Yeah, we're good," I said to Slater and he visibly relaxed. My response must have ticked whatever mental picture he had in his head about control and command.

He turned to the Dickhead. "You have it?" he asked.

The Dickhead turned to me. Suddenly I could see the small lines of tension on the sides of his jaw and the tiny crow's feet on the sides of his eyes. So. Dissatisfied. I decided.

"You will look at it?" he asked. His voice clipped.

"Of course. Those are my rules."

"And if I ask you not to?"

"No can do."

"I am paying."

"And I am delivering. My guess is this information is vital. Like all the information I am asked to deliver."

He nodded. "It's more than that," he said, "More than that. This," he took out a tiny USB drive, "is one of its kind. There is no other record of it. Anywhere."

Out of the corner of my eye I could see the stiffness in the Secret Service goons. They were listening. This meant something to them. What though, I wondered. Slater too. He was stiffer than he should be.

WTF? I mean, it's just a delivery job. I've had in my hands information that could have been exchanged for millions. And all it had cost to the sender and receiver was a measly $40K. Split, usually, I understood. Though not always.

"Should anything happen to it – "

"Look," I cut him off and he looked surprised. Not used to being cut off, perhaps. "This is my job. I see it. Assess it.

Then I deliver it. I am the only one with the decryption key. Should anything happen to me the information stays dead. Everyone's safe. Except me, I guess. But that's why you're paying me."

It was my prepared sales spiel and I'd delivered it so many times that Wendy used to make fun of me.

"What if you're caught?" The Dickhead asked.

"What?"

"What if they capture you?"

"Who will?"

"I don't know. A hypothetical they. And they torture you?"

"Hypothetically?"

"No, no, for real. What if they capture you and torture you so you give them the information."

"Well, they can have it I suppose. Before the torture starts," Dickhead looked at me like I'd gone crazy. Slater too. "It won't do them any good," I added. "They need the decryption key and I don't have that,"

"Who has?"

"No one. That's the beauty of my set up. I have an AI generated, truly random decryption key that is only accessible to me when I reach my destination. The only way to access it is to have my phone at that destination. My phone works off the same GPS coordinates I will input once you tell where I am going with all this."

"So," said Dickhead. He wasn't getting it.

"The only way to decrypt it is to take it where it's supposed to go. To deliver it in other words. The hypothetical kidnappers who will torture me will have to deliver it for me, too."

"I see." Dickhead said.

Slater was taking this in. He'd never heard me explain it in so much detail. To be fair, I never needed to in the past.

"Ok, then." He offered the USB drive to me.

I took it.

3 – The Data

When everything is data nothing can remain a secret. Consider this truth: everything is recorded, somewhere. This means that in order to find out what you want you only need three things: means, motive and opportunity. Just like a crime.

Opportunity in this context really means access and access requires power. Power is either contacts or money. Sometimes both.

That's it. Anyone telling you the world is different is selling you a lie. I am sure you'll choose to buy it because it will help you sleep better at night but that doesn't change the reality you live in. Heck. The reality we all live in.

Everything leaves a trail. Even attempts to erase data are actions which themselves can be tracked.

Can you hide in all this? Sure you can. You can choose to be small. Minnows are usually invisible, until eaten, I guess. You can choose to be irrelevant. Drop out of the grid. Unplug yourself completely. No credit cards. No phones. No TV. No utility bills, which means no utilities. Live off the land and fend for yourself.

I know you're thinking what I am thinking: completely and utterly unrealistic, unless you want to die young of course.

Or, you can make sure they're all looking elsewhere. When everything is data the data that gets noticed is the one that sticks out.

Think about that for a moment. And, BTW, don't let the fact that I am narrating this now lull you into a false sense of security that I got out of it OK. I too, am a piece of data. And though I tried to make sure I didn't raise any red flags, this is not how things went down.

"Before you put that in there you need to make sure everything's unplugged," said Slater. He jumped in the moment I tried to plug the USB drive in and access the data.

"OK, I'm not a newbie to this, you know. This laptop is not connected."

He nodded quickly, flashed a quick look to Dickhead who was still just hovering above me.

Data can tell you a lot just by what it is. Its formatting, provenance, date and time, the form it takes. As a matter of fact data screams information at you as soon as you look at it. This is what makes the world such a frightening place. It's like there is no room to hide any more. No room for secrets.

I transferred the file, opened it.

There were images. Satellite shots of places along with telemetry data with time stamps and GPS details. A house. More like a ranch. More GPS details. Pictures taken throughout the day.

Seen from outer space the main drive showed cars arriving and leaving at various times of the day. Everything time-stamped. Initials marked each photograph, or rather the car it showed.

I looked at it carefully gauging its import. Espionage? Not on a ranch, but you never know. Surveillance of some kind, obviously. This was satellite data and the only ones who were capable of that kind of surveillance were state-level actors.

So, I was a U.S. government stooge now. Great. I briefly wondered whether the initials stenciled in each picture were car occupants or surveillance operatives but it didn't matter. There were a couple of images of people going in and out of the house. A few more time-stamped surveillance shots from beyond the sky.

"Seen enough?" Dickhead couldn't keep quiet. Throughout my check of the data he'd been pacing nervously.

Pausing only to look at me as I scrolled through al the information.

"It's not illegal," Slater said at last.

I nodded. I knew both wanted me to just encrypt it and get ready to deliver it. Yet they were willing to pay $40K for it. I reserved the right to know what I was carrying.

"Not illegal," Dickhead repeated. In my experience when something like that is said emphatically twice, the exact opposite is true.

"OK. Not illegal," I murmured. The satellite images had some kind of serial number. My guess was that they would identify the specific satellite that took them, though given the GPS coordinates that would be superfluous. All one had to do was go back and triangulate to see which of our eyes in the sky was at that point in time. It's an incontrovertible law of physics that two physical objects of roughly the same mass cannot occupy the same point in space and time.

"We good?" Slater asked to fill the void. His cinema talk persona was beginning to get annoying, but I let it slide.

"What's the destination?" I asked.

"Eh?"

"Where am I taking this?"

"Ah,"

I looked at the Dickhead directly for the first time. His eyes, I noted, were big, the pupils slightly dilated. Speed? Cocaine? There were chemicals involved here, for sure. It would explain his monosyllabic answers.

"You have an address you want this delivered to?" I asked.

"Yeah, yes. Yes." He looked at Slater for assistance.

Slater, reached into an inner pocket in his suit. Took out a piece of paper. Placed it carefully on the desk, directly in front of me.

4 – The Address

New York is not one of the world's most iconic cities for nothing. For a start it has that stellar movie presence. Million upon millions can recite some of its streets, know where Manhattan and Staten Island are, know about The Bronx and some even know about TriBeCa.

Standing for "triangle below canal street" TriBeCa which has since lost all its capitalization apart from the first letter, has been gentrified to the point that it is the most expensive neighborhood in New York City.

Approximately 12 miles separate The Bronx from Tribeca. Or better put approximately 12 miles separated my apartment from the residential address I was expected to deliver the encrypted information to.

Twelve miles. If you divide it into 40K you get just over $3k per mile. Not a bad job, I can almost hear you say. I say "almost" because I know you wouldn't say that. You wouldn't. You're far too smart to say that.

You know, as well as I do, that information that costs so much per mile just to deliver has cost a heck of a lot more to acquire. Some one wants it badly and some one else or rather some one else times many times over.

It's why I charge what I charge. Not too much. Not too little either. Enough to be feasible and, also, to filter the wheat from the chaff. Anyone willing to pay $20K upfront is already serious about their data.

"That's just down the road," I say to Slater. Quite literally, the address is less than half an hour by car. I have no idea how long it'd taken Slater's client to get to my place and at what cost to the taxpayer. Then he paid me what I asked to hand deliver what they could have done themselves.

It doesn't take a genius to put two and two together and realize something doesn't quite add up.

"Will you do it?" Slater asked.

The Secret Service goons looked really tense at that point. Afterwards I'd wonder what would have happened had I, at that moment in time, weighed up all the odds and simply said "no'. But I didn't have all the data necessary to make that decision and $40K is a lot of money to say no to, especially when you already have half of it sitting in your account.

Besides I really wanted them out of my place. Fast.

"Sure, I'll do it," I said and everyone appeared to relax.

***

I have a ritual I go through before each run. I don't know why I do it and it used to drive Wendy crazy but I know that without it I just don't feel right during a run.

I take a shower. Hot and long. Then I shave. I shave my face, my chest, my arms. My armpits. I dress in black. Black cargo trousers, loose fit so I can run if necessary. Black tank top. Black tee on top. Black, lace up leather boots with rugged, flat soles. Steel toe cap. If it's winter I have a black scarf and black leather jacket.

Psychologists and, these days, neuroscientists; talk a lot about enclothed cognition. We'd like to think that the clothes don't make the man (or woman) but unfortunately, they do. The part we dress up is the part we end up enacting.

The idea of transforming ourselves into someone else, something else, via the sheer act of dressing up releases neurochemicals in our brain that enable higher executive functions to come fully into play.

If I could get away with it I'd dab a little undereye black like football players, but I can't. So I don't. I finish the part I am getting into by adding a black-on-black data phone and a black wrist cuff watch with a broad leather band.

Then, once I have downloaded the data into my phone, destroyed all the copies and encrypted it, I am good to go.

So, you will ask me now, what exactly is this part you play? What sort of character do you slip into while getting dressed up this way?

Honestly, I can't answer this completely. Not because I don't want tom but because I don't really know. Whatever atavistic part of me drives me to dress up this way feels more comfortable with high risks and rewards than I, plain old, simple, everyday Alex Logan will ever do.

No, really. Ask me to do a job and I assess it from every direction. I will ask for as much data as possible. I weigh things up, think of the risks, look at the data and try to divine whether someone would really give sufficient fucks about it to kill another human being for it. Or worse.

Yeah. There are worse things than dying. Believe me.

But the black-clad Alex me is different. He understands the risks and rewards but he cares about things differently. To Black-Alex the world is a place of patterns where nodes and edges constantly rub against each other.

Black-Alex sees data and he sees metadata. The girl in the mini-skirt crossing the street is a data node to him. He assesses her in terms of attractiveness, confidence, beauty. Then he reads the metadata: the clothes she wears and their cost. The direction of her travel. Her degree of awareness of her surroundings. All of this means something. The way she reaches for her phone the moment it rings and the way she scans the crowd around her as she talks to the person who rang her. It all means something.

That version of me is wired. Jacked on the sheer ability to see and understand. Intelligence is the sexiest thing on the planet. It is the ultimate power trip. It guarantees you nothing beyond the rush of the moment and the feeling that you can see exactly what will happen within a specific, bounded data set.

That's it.

Yet, like the best drug on the planet it keeps you deep in its embrace, unable to give it up. Unable to move on. Realizing your potential folly and yet, just like the Oracle at the Temple of Apollo in Delphi, hoping that your interpretation is the correct one, that the metadata you've read truly reveals the hidden picture you've been looking for; so now you understand.

That Alex is amazing.

No screwing up anything. Super-capable. Hyper-focused. The superlatives roll off my tongue here because it doesn't feel like I am praising myself. It feels like I am truly praising someone else. The ghost of something that takes me over and makes me feel the most alive I've ever felt.

Black-Alex is addicted to hyper-realism. Because he feels every bit of data his sensorium feels virtually overwhelmed. I am not sure there has ever been a thing called "high on reality" that's legit, but if there ever was, well this has to be it and Alex has to be patient zero. Addict number one.

"So, tiger." I say into the bathroom mirror reflection of myself. The edges are still fuzzy with the condensed droplets of cooling steam and the visage staring back at me appears to come from the center of some featureless, formless abyss. A well of potentialities that take sudden form.

Me. Now.

I take a deep breath and already the tingling in my spine has begun. I feel every air molecule. Every surge and ebb of the steam in my bathroom.

Naked, I walk to the bedroom leaving damp footprints on the floor behind. Wendy would have laughed at that back then when laughter was something we still did together.

"Ghost walker," she said once, looking at my footprints. The early days when I started data running and the money seemed to be incredible and coming out of nowhere. "You're like a ghost walker,"

"Ghosts don't have feet," I said. I was actually trying to remember whether there was an official line on that. "They kinda float just above ground,"

"You have a citation for that?" she asked in her most cheeky voice.

Citation. I turned around and slapped her ass. She was wearing jeans. Tight. A white cotton top that was cut a little too low. She smacked me right back. Her hand making a loud sound on my bare bum and then we were rolling around the floor, our embrace making us forget where each of us begun and the other one ended.

Ghost walker.

I snapped back to the present. The tingling still there. Rising as I dressed. There was a coldness descending inside me. With Wendy gone the job was all I had. And sometimes I didn't even know why I had it, why I still did all this, except it was I felt important to still do something.

"So. Ready?" my reflection smiled back the answer. In the bedroom mirror I stood like a dark angel. A figure dressed in black.

I checked my phone where all the data was. Brand-new. Never used. The number was routed through several different VPNs to get to me via Bangladesh. Though I was, at that moment, in Manhattan, the bill would go to a trader address in a small village with no internet and a strong trade in goat milk and cheese.

That Alex, there, was a ghost. A made-up presence that existed only in the virtual domain of bills and balances and costs and data plans.

"Ready." I affirmed to myself. I checked the lacing on my boots one last time. And then, with the finality of a man who is going on a mission from which he may never come back, I stepped over the threshold and locked the door behind me.

5 – On Foot

Everything needs a reason to happen. Most times the reasons aren't evident. Make this a life lesson for you. I was steeped deep in the self-generated myth of my work persona. I felt empowered, knowledgeable, determined, focused and untouchable.

Getting to my destination from my apartment was a series of decisions. Every decision, of course, represented a choice. Each choice, I knew, would have consequences.

My destination was across the Harlem River. Wikipedia (if you care to look) will tell you that the "although walking speeds can vary greatly depending on many factors such as height, weight, age, terrain, surface, load, culture, effort, and fitness, the average human walking speed at crosswalks is about 5.0 kilometres per hour (km/h), or about 1.4 meters per second (m/s), or about 3.1 miles per hour (mph)."

Google maps probably took that into their primary point of calculation when they presented me with my 4hr 16 minute delivery time if I took 5th Avenue. It was a path with many left and right turns to begin with any some small adjustments but most of it was pretty straightforward.

Data, to paraphrase Stewart Brand, wants to be free. It also wants to be expensive. I was, right at that moment, carrying data that was already expensive that did not want to be free. But that, of course, is a self-delusional lie. Data, just like information, on its own doesn't want to do anything. It is inert, like a stone. But just like a stone, once picked up, it becomes rife with potential. It can be used to build amazing constructs. Or it can be loaded onto catapults and used as an instrument of death and destruction.

Data can do anything we want it to because it is the building block of our actions, which means it is a clear signal of our intent. Our world is made of data and, if quantum physicists are correct, so is the universe. It is nothing more but data, encoded, I guess, in different energy formats.

I walked as I thought. The geometric brownstone buildings outside, the broad pavements and parked cars on either side, all formed part of a pattern of existence. A familiar anchor that gave me a sense of control.

This was important to me. It should be important to you too. We're all locked into this journey where we wake up each day uncertain of what is going to happen next. There are so many potential outcomes to each and every event around us that rightly we should be paralyzed with fear.

Our worst nightmares are but a click away. We fool ourselves of course with predictions based upon our certain knowledge of the past. We tell to ourselves that the past is a predictor of the future and if things happened in a specific way back then and we already have concrete, irrefutable and direct sensory evidence that they did, then they will continue to happen in the exact same way in the future. Indefinitely.

That is a pipedream. We need it. The familiarity of the scene outside my apartment block became, for me, the means I used to control the uncertainty I felt.

Since I became alone I've felt more and more of that uncertainty. The anxiety that comes with putting things in motion, allowing the trajectory of specific events to take its course. Lead to whatever momentum the specificities of the attributes each moment possesses, leads to. You get in a tank and press the pedal for moving forward and any vehicle on your path is subject to the inevitability of physics governed by a superior mass of metal that's now hurtling towards it.

Simples.

There were a couple of dog walkers. A woman holding a closed umbrella. It was odd as there is no chance of rain. Not today. I checked. An old man shuffling alone, taking a walk. His head held low. His mind lost in its own thoughts.

I took all this in at a glance. The buzzed-up Alex I'd become assessing everything, checking to see if something was already out of joint. Out of place.

No parked vans with blacked-out windows anywhere. That was a good thing. No suspicious cars. No one looking at me funny or for longer than it took to ascertain that I too lived here and therefore I belonged.

So, Alex, I told myself. You will get this a lot now. My Black-Alex persona talks to itself in the third person. You may find it disturbing but psychologists will tell you it is a healthy thing to do. A mind under stress, distances itself from the stressors it experiences therefore attaining mental and emotional equilibrium by referring to itself in the third person and coolly appraising the facts that surround it and the situation it is in.

No predicament just yet, of course. But you already know one is coming. At least one. And that means that my current smart talk notwithstanding I am due to make a stupid decision and some bad choices fairly soon.

But right this minute, the first decision, the one that maybe set so many other things in motion, was to walk the distance.

My choice. My reasons: the distance was short. Walking allowed me time to think. Enjoy the job, as it were. It also meant that I was harder to track. Cars have electronics. Their journey is predetermined because they can only use the road network and, within that, a very specific, predetermined part of it, in order to get from point A to point B. Heck you don't even need to track them much to know where they are and where they are going.

Plus, occupants are trapped. Handily imprisoned in a metal box that can only go as fast as traffic and traffic lights allow it to.

On foot on the other hand I was fluid. I could change direction at any time. Choose to go in, through or round buildings. My speed was my own.

For the distance involved, the job at hand, required nothing less.

George Crabbe, an early Victorian Poet who wrote in heroic couplets, had a line describing *The Borrough*:

> *Cities and towns, the various haunts of men,*
> *Require the pencil; they defy the pen:*

Like most Victorians he was a little bit of a cipher. A surgeon, a poet and, as it turned out, a clergyman. Quite an unusual set of skills, you might think. He was right though about where we live. Neighborhoods are strange. Fixed and fluid at the same time. Schrodinger's "dead and alive" principle in action.

Everything appears still. Fixed in time. Frozen. Dead, perhaps. But under the surface everything is moving. People and relationships. Lives and dreams. Decisions and choices. We are all like water.

I kept checking the street as I walked. My eyes carefully taking in each object. Each car. Each pedestrian I passed. The traffic and the time of day. It all tallied. Made sense. Told me that I, Black-Alex, had nothing to worry about.

Everything was kosher. Which is why, as I walked towards Van Nest Avenue and my first right hand turn I made a conscious decision to stop by the El Paso Deli on the right and gram a sandwich. Van Nest is mostly residential here. Trees line the streets. It is about as idyllic as any large city neighborhood can ever be.

Margarita was behind the counter. Her long black hair pulled back into a bun and covered with a hairnet. She was maybe 25. Pretty. With black, shiny eyes and a full smile that made me feel good inside every time I saw it.

"Hey Alex," she said when she saw me.

"Margarita," I smiled back at her, "bella chica en esta sala,"

She smiled back at my attempt with Spanish. "Gracias buen señor" she said back smoothly and then switched to English. "Of course there are no other women in this place so your compliment is a little double-edged," she let out a small giggle at my expression.

"Of course, I meant this city," I shot back.

"Stick to English hombre," she said.

It was my turn to laugh. "Any sandwiches left?"

"For you Alex, always. You know that." She took in my outfit. "You working?"

"Yeah. I have a little job to do. Making sure I don't run out of fuel,"

"You need a good woman to look after you," she said and then remembered my situation. "Oh-"

"It's Ok," I cut her off. Kept the smile on to show there was no harm done. The playful mood however had gone. She turned to gran a sandwich for me.

"Pastrami as usual?" she asked, her hands busy picking one and getting a bag.

"Yeah," I nodded. "And a drink, Red Bull or something."

"OK," she placed both in a bag for me. I thanked her.

"Muchas gracias hermosa niña," I said.

She beamed. "You'll need to learn some proper Spanish at some point Alex, leave off this Google Translate stuff,"

"Language is just data." I answered, paying her.

"No, no, no," she quickly shot back. She reached across the counter to pass me my change. "Language is feelings. Words have passion. Inflexion, intonation."

She was right. Data had context. Metadata changed their meaning. This is why machines find language so hard to do right.

"Margarita, I might have to buy you dinner some time," I said, "Get your help with these Spanish words,"

"You keep promising," she flirted back.

Yeah, she was right. I did. Words had lost some of their intent for me. I saw them as more a channel of communication that was based on raw data instead of feelings.

I curtsied towards her to show my appreciation. She smiled back. I turned and stepped back outside. Nothing had changed. Nothing.

Then, my phone rang.

***

Events that people normally expect are clashed as "normal". They are given that designation because understanding what they mean is obvious. Everything signifies something and nothing takes place in a vacuum.

When you understand these rules of everyday conduct you understand most of what you have to do in order to respond which means that you also begin to understand how you should function.

People feel lost sometimes. Unsure of what to do. That's because life comes without a roadmap. There's no rule book. As a result most of it is a mystery to us until it becomes "afterwards". By then it's in our past. The past is a poor guide when it comes to the future. It only tends to lock us into what we've done before and if we've done very little then, there you have it.

The phone rang again.

When I am on a job, I'm off the grid. Each phone I use is new. The calls routed through a complex network that has me based elsewhere.

No local SIM card. No internet signal. I need to be untraceable. I still need eyes and ears. I pay others for that.

I picked up on the third ring. "Yeah,"

"Something's up." The voice was male. Not one I knew, but then again, I don't need to know all the voices of those I pay to do specific tasks.

"Be more specific."

"The dude, your client. That asshole's name you sent us to keep tabs on."

"Yeah,"

"He just went dark."

"Explain."

"Off-the-grid dark. Cellphone off. No GPS of his car. No reply on home address call. No emails. Dark. Like he'd shut down."

I thought for a moment, weighing the meaning of that. Home was still just around the corner. I could just, literally, turn around and go back. Use a hammer to smash the phone I had and all the information in it. "You tried landlines?"

"We tried everything! No reply. Dude has three homes across the US. There must be staff. No one's picking up."

"Weird,"

"I know, right?" the voice sounded more excited than worried. Then again why should he be worried. The client was mine. There were only connections leading to me. Maybe.

"How long?" I asked.

"What?"

"How long ago did this happen?"

There was a pause as he calculated. "Ten, maybe fifteen minutes ago."

About the time I left my apartment, I thought. Give or take. The first rule of data running is that there are no coincidences. Everything has a reason, even if you can't quite see it. The second rule is that there are no random events. Everything is linked to everything else which means that the things that trigger something are connected to other things, somewhere.

When you're at the fringes of the network. Or not really doing anything that can affect it, it does require some pretty amazing amount of bad luck to be affected by something that doesn't involve you.

It really does not happen that often.

All other times you are "in it", because you happened to have done something.

"Dark all at once?"

"I don't know. It's only me on Watch right now. You're the only case. I checked sequentially so I don't know the order it happened."

He was smart. He understood what I was asking. The way something like a disconnect happens is a reveal. Did the landlines go out first? Then the cell phones? Did it happen the other way around? The gap of time between specific events is also a reveal. Right now I had nothing. I made a decision.

"Keep checking," I said. "Let me know what you find and, can you keep tabs on this line. Now?"

Again that pause as he analyzed what I was asking. Smart. Like I said.

"How far out?"

"Three layers. See if anyone is out there looking for me and," now I paused, though it was mostly for effect: "you." I finished.

He took it on board. Barely paused this time. "Will do." He hang up.

It takes a very special person to know with real confidence when the conversation with a stranger is over. I bit into my sandwich and turned down Van Nest Avenue heading towards the White Plains Road intersection. The pastrami, I thought was really quite good. Already I was looking forward to the taste of cold Red Bull to wash it down with.

6 – News

Walking creates a different perspective. Cars find it hard to tail you. Going at your speed gives the game away. Pedestrians soon become conspicuous. That leaves drones.

Chewing on the last of my pastrami sandwich I chugged down the Red Bull. Everything in Black Alex's world is a symbol of some sorts that has some kind of connotation that acts as a trigger.

Red Bull is no exception. The stimulant in it is caffeine. I mean I should have probably got a double Espresso and it might have had more of a kick, but Red Bull delivered it cold, with calories behind it and I've always felt it made my brain pop.

I'd only got as far as the United Methodist Church, opposite the STEAM Bridge School, the area was truly residential, and my phone rang.

I picked up immediately. "Yeah,"

"Problems," the same male voice as before said.

"Speak,"

"It's not just your client that's gone dark. It's also his detail."

"What?"

"I thought I'd track them. Find him through them. They are Secret Service. Their location is known at all times. They have secure comms they call in on. Plus their GPS signal. Plus one additional tracking device, Not sure who had that,"

"And?"

"All dark. Same time as your client. And the GPS on their cars." He paused and let everything sink in.

It probably meant some kind of catastrophic failure on their network, I thought. Added: "Have you checked to see if any other teams are experiencing the same issues?"

You check to see if the problem is known. If it is, which means others have experienced it, then it's not unique. Just annoying. Not sinister. Just plain, old, human clusterfuck.

"Yes, I did," said the voice, "Everyone checks out."

"Everyone?"

"I could only get details on three teams in such a short time," he explained. One three blocks away from your client and his team. If it was a network issue they'd be running off the same nodes more or less. They weren't affected."

Ergo, no network issue. "Good work," I said. Heard a soft grunt of acknowledgement. "Keep monitoring. Let me know what is happening, the moment it happens."

"OK." The connection went dead.

Was I in trouble? I honestly didn't know. The data I had hadn't appeared that valuable. But you never know with data. There's another issue that can cloud the waters a lot. The value of data is contextual. I, at that moment, had no idea who it belonged to and who it was intended for. Both of these things changed the picture.

I looked for a bin to throw away the sandwich wrapper and the bag with the now empty can of Red Bull. As I did so I scanned the street around me, looked at all the cars on the road. Not that many this time of day.

On impulse I turned and headed for the Church. I had plenty of time to kill and the nagging suspicion that I was missing something. Something important.

You can't do everything fast and do it well. I was scanning the traffic, checking the street and trying to work out the problem I was having. My brain was splitting its resources to cover everything and it wasn't working out. I needed a little respite. The Church would be quiet, I guessed.

It was empty.

Guess midday is not the best time of day for the faithful to commune with their Creator. I know what you're thinking. Shitty comment. Yeah. It was meant to be.

I have no faith. I am coming clean so there are no surprises.

A simple crucifix adorned the far wall. I found a seat in the middle. That way, should anyone walk in behind me I'd have plenty of space to maneuver. As a precaution I put my phone on vibrate.

I sat there, in the quiet of the Church, on my own; gathering my thoughts. I was in total just over 150m from home. That's barely 160 yards. I'd had a pastrami sandwich, drunk a can of Red Bull and had, for the first time ever, received a call from the Watchers I'd hired to tell me that maybe, just maybe, I was out of a client.

If that doesn't sound weird to you then nothing will. But weird, as the online edition of the Cambridge English Dictionary will tell you is: "very strange and unusual, unexpected, or not natural".

Strange, unusual, unexpected or not natural. Welcome to my life since Wendy – I stopped the thought before it bloomed and focused instead on the facts at hand.

I had very little go on with and weird is weird only in retrospect. In real life weird happens incrementally. The modern day, real-life equivalent of the boiling frog experiment which, incidentally, is a myth. But then you knew that already, didn't you?

Still, it makes for a great analogy. A graphic depiction of how horrible things can go from not-so-horrible to horrible incrementally with us barely noticing as long as the increments are small enough to ignore.

In psychology they call this the Overton Window and although they tend to apply it mostly in the realm of public discourse where mores and expectations are guided by tradition rather than written rules, it is applicable to pretty much every other part of life where incremental change sneaks things onto us that we should never put up with.

What was playing predominantly at the back of my mind that day however were the lyrics from the Mamas and the Papas from *California Dreaming* where the lines kept repeating themselves in my psyche:

> *Stopped into a church*
> *I passed along the way*
> *Well, I got down on my knees*
> *Got down on my knees*
> *And I pretend to pray*
> *I pretend to pray*

Wendy used to love the band and its catchy signature tunes would play in the background of our flat most days on the Sonos. I wondered a couple of things as I sat there then: First, had I stopped here out of affectation? Were my actions guided by the cinematic desire for melodrama and a sense of movie-style romance? Second, would I have stopped here had I not first bought a sandwich which kinda slowed me down and made me feel all nice and fuzzy inside?

Free will is an illusion. Most times we respond to environmental stimuli that makes us do something over something else. We think we choose but really the decisions are made for us long before we become conscious of them.

Was I really in danger? Was I in trouble?

Honestly, sitting there, back then I didn't know. Had no way of knowing. I was 20K richer, well, 15K if you count the fee paid to the Watchers. A client going dark was metadata but metadata needed to be interpreted, so what it meant was up for grabs.

I could go full-on paranoid and decide that something was fishy and I needed to now get in front of it or get out. Or, I could put everything down to nothing. Clients could choose to do whatever the hell they wanted to do and certainly this asshole of a client I had neither picked, nor solicited but whom I had, nevertheless, agreed to do business with; could go to Hell and back for all I really cared.

As long as I got paid.

Now, that was something that focused the mind and added some extra motivation.

Money, they will tell you with a smile, makes the world go round. The "they" I imagine in my mental picture telling you this are neither very smart nor very original. Money doesn't make the world go round. The physical laws of the universe do that. But money is a motive force because it is the means through which we go from a situation where we may be unhappy to another one where we may be less unhappy.

See? Amoebas after all. Just vying for different type of food than our unicellular organism. I was not immune to the motive force of money. Particularly what it could buy. So my decision making process, at that stage, was of the sort I would call normal.

To illustrate the situation I need to use colors. If you and I were sat together right now and I was explaining all this to you I'd need a Whiteboard and four markers going from White to Yellow to Orange to Red. Ok, Ok, I know there is no real white ink, especially on a Whiteboard but for the purpose of illustrating my argument suppose there was.

These is the classic color scheme created by United States Marine Lieutenant Colonel Jeff Cooper to guide an individual in the use of sidearms, pistols.

Col. Cooper was in WWII and what he witnessed there in many active deployments some of which required brutal hand-to-hand combat was that those who survived weren't necessarily the best in terms of shooting proficiency but rather the ones who were better mentally prepared.

It was a sort of warming-up of the brain that allowed it to better allocate resources to deal with extremely adversarial situations and help the person survive.

His color scheme then goes from White which, as you might have guessed, means that everything is hanky-dory all the way up to red where you pretty much need to be ready to fight for your life.

Cooper perfected this as a guideline for army use of pistols and it's become a kind of sidearms bible which instructors absolutely love. Were it not for neuroscience we'd be able to write Cooper off as some kind of cuckoo gun-nut who thrived on reasons to carry and use pistols.

Unfortunately neuroscience stepped in and discovered that the human brain, despite its versatility, is piss-poor at doing anything fast or responding to situations that require critical thinking, snap judgement and fast action. Which is why the color scheme actually works. The brain functions best if it can correctly identity the situation so that it can start prepping itself.

So, there I was. In a Church pretending to pray, thinking whether I was over-reacting and imagining danger where none existed. It's a cognitive trap we can fall into that's guided by perception.

Perception is the filter we apply to interpret the data we collect from the world around us and create what we call "Reality". My sensorium, at that moment, was both remote and constrained.

Constrained because the data dribbling in was negligible. Too little to infer much without thinking that I was imagining things. Remote out of necessity which meant that the Watchers would only call in as necessary and what they deemed to be necessary was also an issue.

Because I was aware of all of this I felt relatively relaxed and competent. My sense of my own knowledge and capability blinding me to the urgency of the moment and making me feel that truly there was nothing I couldn't cope with because I had prepared for virtually anything.

None of these two assumptions was really true. But finding that out was going to take time. So, unaware of my predicament. Acting with a color code of White when really I should already be on Yellow and maybe, even Orange, I stepped out of the Church into the street that was now beginning to pick up traffic.

As a precaution I changed the setting on my phone, setting the ring back on but the choosing a low tone and vibration as an alert. Stupid, maybe, but I was cautious even when I wasn't cautious enough.

Wendy's favorite tune was playing at the back of my mind and I was thinking, also, just how much fun we had in the beginning. When we'd just moved into this Bronx apartment and felt that the world was now, finally, ours.

7 – Space

Everyone needs a place to call home. We feel that as a necessity. It's our equivalent of our cave. The place where we can drop the mask we're forced to wear and let our hair down and feel our depleted energy sources replenish themselves.

We hadn't always lived there. Wendy and I had grown up in the city's poorest neighborhood of Morrisania and Crotona in the Bronx, where 44 percent of the residents live below the federal poverty level—the highest poverty rate in the city.

It is the petri dish of an uncompromising reality. The place where the handy soundbites and sleek slogans of "Just say no" and "crime doesn't pay" become the meaningless background noise against which a very real sense of urgency and survival play out.

Without money even getting food becomes problematic. Without a regular food supply each day is fraught with stress. It leads to increasingly risky behavior which then leads to the kind of statistics politicians call "problematic".

We clawed and fought to get out of there. I met Wendy when she was 19. Etching her designs and trying to find takers in a digital world where the global economy meant she could be undercut by someone living in Bangladesh and earning, each day, even less than her.

See how competition makes everything instantly better? At the extreme poverty and hunger end of the scale it leads to a race to the bottom as those of us born in the wrong family, the wrong address, the wrong neighborhood, vie with each other for scraps and aim to survive just one more day.

I learnt to code. Made apps. Wrote website code for email newsletters. I taught myself. Went through law school on the proceeds. Dreamt big. Had big dreams.

Data. All that should have taught us something. Me. It should have taught me something. But sometimes the lessons we need to learn in order to survive come too late.

It took us ten years to get out of that neighborhood and find somewhere where the sound of firing came from the occasional car engine backfire, rather than a weapon being aimed and fired.

That kind of personal journey builds character. That's what those who live in Tribeca 10007 will tell you. The average annual income in the ZIP code is $879,000, Hagan and Lu reported. Beyoncé, Jay-Z, and Taylor Swift have apartments in the district with price tags in the range of $30 million.

Character.

The word the rich use every time they want to tell the poor that the world is exactly the way it should be and they have to know their place in it.

It's ironic they needed me to run their data.

While I was quick to see the irony I was not so quick to remember where I'd come from. The sheer effort of the horror of my past led my mind to build a convenient wall around it.

It took an act of monumental stupidity and rage to breach it. Or rather an act of pain.

We conveniently forget the pain.

Amoebas. We act to get away from the pain-zone and move towards the no-pain zone. Tell me again about Free Will. When was the last time you chose to remain in a state where all you felt was pain?

I was heading towards Tribeca and 10007.

Cognitive dissonance is a killer. Ask any therapist. He'd tell you that it's "the state of having inconsistent thoughts, beliefs, or attitudes, especially as relating to behavioral decisions and attitude change."

It's more than that. Neuroscientists know that in a state of cognitive dissonance there is considerable "mental stress (discomfort) experienced by a person who simultaneously holds two or more contradictory beliefs, ideas, or values (i.e., when performing an action that contradicts one of those beliefs, ideas, or values; or when confronted with new information that contradicts one of those beliefs, ideas, and values)."

What makes it particularly destructive, they will tell you, is the fact that cognitive dissonance affects both resting-state and decision-related activity of the prefrontal cortex, which monitors internal conflicts and mistakes. It affects most those who have a higher level of self-organization because it disrupts the patterns of their very existence.

Cognitive dissonance is a killer in an almost literal sense. The gate of the Van Nest Park was open as I passed and, acting on impulse, I entered it.

I found a bench to sit on. The park is small. Trees line its fenced perimeter, throwing a deep shade. Flower beds run in-between. Stepping stones form convenient walkways and there is a variety of shrubs and bushes.

It's one small lung in a neighborhood where there is a lot of concrete. It has its own ecosystem. Birds and bees. Butterflies and weevils. I know this in not any great detail because Wendy used to talk about it in those terms.

I have a memory of us sitting in the park, in those early days when everything was alright. And she'd lie back on the bench and rest her head on my lap and look up at the sky she could see through the canopy of the trees, high overhead.

"Ten more years?" she'd ask.

The question of where we were heading. Where it was all going.

"Ten more years," I'd say absent-mindedly. My mind thinking about code.

I should have treasured those moments more. Paid more attention. Watched for the minutiae that are the metadata of a relationship whose ties are weakening, whose passion is evaporating, whose cast of two is now becoming uncertain.

My thoughts played out like a movie in the screen of my mind. And I knew, even as I replayed some of it, all of it, that none of it could be trusted with any degree of accuracy.

Memories are fluid. Some get erased. Others get written in, even if they're not our own. The constant narrative of our identity is a movie that plays all the time and its demands require that the background sets, the special effects, the moments of drama and suspense, conform to the script in play at that moment in time.

I tried to remember what Wendy had been wearing when she lay on the bench and rested her head on my lap and couldn't. A singular inability that made the whole memory suddenly suspect.

Had it happened at all? I certainly remember it as words and expressions. Wendy smiling dreamily as she looked up at the sky but she'd never been quite as carefree and dreamy as my mental recollection of her made her out to be.

She'd always been a little highly strung. Disappointment about something was hidden deep in her. She was in a constant state of anxiety and agitation. She wanted us to move on and on, do better and better and do it, like yesterday.

In our relationship she drove me harder than I drove myself.

We'd been here a few times. How many? I couldn't remember. Another inconsistency? Maybe? I mean who counts the number of times they visit a local park?

We'd been here. That was certain. We'd sat on a bench. Which one? It now became important I remember that. I looked around anxious to recreate the viewing angle of my mental projection of that not too-distant memory. There was another bench a little to my right, opposite where I was sat down.

I changed positions to sit on it. Looked around. I could see the traffic through the black mental railings of the park. The cars flashing between the odd bush or shrub used to create cover. I looked up at the sky. The time was important but I had no way of recreating that. I cursed myself for not paying attention.

Wendy and I had sat here. I was sure of that. She had smiled. That too I remembered clearly. My right hand was on her stomach, palm flat as she lay on her back. She'd touched the back of it with both of hers. My left hand was on her left shoulder, touching it lightly, forming a cradle of sorts for her head on my lap.

It was clear. Clear.

What was she wearing? A Tee. No. A long-sleeved summer top?

I wasn't sure. The memory hovered tantalizingly close but existing in the in-between place that the mind has for what is exists between recall and fabrication.

Was I making up her story? Our story?

The cars flashing by beyond formed a backdrop of activity that made my stillness all that more poignant.

I could, I thought, star in my very own movie. The hero of a story of a love that's found and lost because its principal protagonists failed to communicate.

I smiled at my idiocy, unaware how that smile looked now on my lips. "Communication. Communication between us is key," I'd said that once, sounding like a family therapist speaking to a client.

Emoting comes difficult to me. "The universe is information," I'd added as if that somehow explained better what I'd said to her. "That's what keeps it together,"

Stupid.

Cars. Flashing. Beyond the rails.

The brain always notices things. It keeps on taking in sensory information from all around. Visual, auditory and tactile. I suddenly felt the play of the sun on my body as the rays stole through the canopy overhead. The leaves, high above me moved because there was a breeze.

The sun was warm. The rays playing against me inconsistent. Now one would fly through. Then another. Traffic moved beyond the park railings. People in cars going about their business.

Cars.

The thing about going on foot is that it makes it really hard for someone to track you, to follow you, without becoming conspicuous that they are doing so.

The brain sees and hears everything. But what it makes you aware of is what you're paying attention to. What you're looking for. That was the secret of Cooper's Color Code really. It sensitized the brain not to the danger that might be around it. That, like everything else, lay in a future whose potential was hard to even guess at.

But it made the brain look for particular things more. And the more it looked the more it saw them. And saw them more easily and earlier so then the one whose brain had done all that had higher chances of survival because he was better prepared.

Trying to track a civilian on foot with cars is stupid. Conspicuous. But he has to be looking for it. His Cooper's Color Code Alert had better be on Orange or Red, otherwise he would miss the obvious. Not because the brain didn't somehow see it. The brain sees everything. But because it didn't recognize the significance of what it'd seen.

Simples. Again.

I hadn't particularly been looking at the traffic because I didn't think there was any need to. But my brain had nevertheless been taking everything in. My eyes had seen.

Through the cars flashing past the railings the sleek vans in black, with blacked out windows stood out. But only if you were looking out for them.

I sat very, very still willing myself not to move. Not to do anything that a regular park goer wouldn't do. The van occupants, I told myself, also suffered from the same blindness induced by not accurately estimating which of Cooper's famous colors to apply to this situation.

For them, I guess, I was still White. An easy mark, barely left home yet. On foot. Which is why they were combing the street trying to find me.

There must have been at least three, no, four vans. Identical apart from the number plates, they were going in a formation of two, several car lengths separating the one in front from the one behind and combing both sides of the street.

Smart. If I happened to see the first and evade it, the second, coming up behind it would pick me up, I thought.

But, also, not so smart. They were combing both sides of the street which meant they weren't too sure which direction I was really heading towards.

My guess was that, right now, they were just a search party operating within a widening spiral to track down a person travelling on foot.

They would, before too long, have to widen their spiral. Increase the periodicity of their appearance. Did they know what I look like? Possibly. What I was wearing? I wasn't too sure.

Obviously they were on the lookout for my appearance. I sank just a little lower in the bench, in the park. And timed the time they took to show up, across my vision.

8 – Run

"This is so James Bond," Wendy had said to me.

My idea. I'd shared it. How data running was the thing. Secure, end-to-end encryption with an unbreakable cipher. The secret was safe.

I'd joked that in this case the only way to kill the secret was to kill the messenger.

"Is it going to be dangerous?" she'd asked.

"Well, it's legal. Or rather the service is legal. The information … I don't know. All data has value. If that value is high enough to someone it could be risky to carry it, I guess."

It'd been a logical guess. If you have something someone else may want it stands to reason that, at some point, they may be prepared to do anything to get it.

That's why I'd learned to be careful. During the run I was invisible. If there were face recognition camera I wore a bandana. Sometimes a cap. I had a couple of handheld lasers rigged into it. The beams were invisible during daytime but face recognition cameras would be blinded by them.

I was offline. Completely. Burner phone with foreign registration and network. No internet during the run. New phone number each time.

Not even the client knew the number. To contact me I always gave them a new manufactured number the Watchers would give me. He'd call them. They would route it through to me.

The Watchers, of course, were the ultimate firewall. Blockchain encryption software and a decentralized cell where each member worked with either the one below him or the one above him. Were they to become compromised the most the organization would lose would be two operatives who knew nothing and had met no one.

Each job had a flat fee: Five thousand dollars. They were worth it for the peace of mind alone but they were also really, really useful. During a data run they were my eyes and ears. They monitored my cell phone signal. Knew my location. Scanned the airwaves for chatter. Plugged into the local police network and the traffic light camera grid on my path. They were my guardian angels protecting me from all evil.

With them having my back I truly felt invincible. Plus I liked the fact that I had never been given their names or knew their faces. They were just voices to me, at the other end of a cell phone connection.

The spiral was widening. The four vans now appeared every 20 minutes. I was impressed by their thoroughness. They were following protocol. Hence the spiral and its periodicity. And they were not tiring. They kept widening it every two rotations.

That meant they were disciplined. Well trained and supervised. Now, I didn't yet know who "they" were but at least I knew they existed.

It did occur to me that this too might have a more innocent explanation. Blacked out vans are not hard to come by. There were other reasons for them to be out there beyond what I do.

That's the problem with probability. It feels very real until you actually look at it closely. Then it kinda evaporates into conjecture and supposition. I have always thought that this is what high-level intelligence work feels like. Everything's based on hunches and hearsay. Metadata and its interpretation. Smokescreens and what they signify.

Logically I had little to go on. In a logical world however there is little room for feelings and, right now, what I was seeing just felt wrong.

My one defense, I thought, was my unpredictability. I'd been on foot and, as luck would have it; or if you prefer, my uniquely unorthodox way of doing things, I'd barely got 600 yards away from home in almost an hour. That was something they just wouldn't expect.

I stayed in my park bench. Hunched low, sinking into myself as much as I possibly could, and dialed the Watchers.

"Yo," the same voice as before. I sighed relief. It meant I wouldn't have to worry about continuity and having to explain my situation to someone new.

"You have some news,"

"Yes, Alex. I was going to call you. I am trying to make sure. We picked up some chatter on the Police scanner. There's an APB out on you for burglary with intent. Plus the report says you might be armed and dangerous,"

"Shit,"

"There's more."

It figured. There always was more. "There's a picture of you. Taken this morning. Dressed in black."

"What?"

"They must have set it up from the very beginning. But why?"

If there was any doubt at all before, if in my mind I'd wished that all of this was some kind of misunderstanding, that somehow those black, unmarked vans with greyed out windows weren't really looking for me, this made it all evaporate.

The "why" of course, as Simon Sinek explained in not one but two very wordy books is at the heart of everything. In my case it was simple enough: data. More specifically the data I had seen, encrypted and now carried. But that didn't mean anything. The data itself could be anything, from a top-level state secret to someone's presence at a house party, recorded via satellite from space.

Without context the data meant nothing.

It was ironic, of course, that whoever was after me had tipped me off just on how important the seemingly meaningless jumble of data I carried actually was.

"I don't yet know why," I confided to the voice. "Maybe I could just call this whole thing off," I didn't mean it. I was just thinking aloud, starting from the option that was least likely to play out.

"I don't think you can do that Alex,"

"Why not?"

There was the briefest of pauses. Then: "They're in your house."

"What?" I was beginning to hate the note of surprise that was creeping in my voice.

"I was waiting to confirm a few things before I called you, so to give you the clearest picture I could,"

At that point I would have gladly hugged whoever the voice belonged to.

"Are they scanning towers?"

"What?"

"Is my cell still clean?"

"Ah, yes. Yes. They are monitoring your own phone. It wasn't at home and it's not on so, I suspect, they're just waiting for a signal from it."

Smart.

"And," he continued "they are in your living room. Waiting. I had to access your home security system to get the feed."

"How did you do that?" I was curious. I thought I had closed all the loopholes in that system.

"I hacked your password," he said, matter-of-factly.

"I see," I was glad I'd chosen the Watchers to watch over me at that moment.

"Can you do me a favor?" I asked.

"You're the client," he said. "You've paid upfront."

I wasn't sure if that was affirmation of censure, so I didn't reply. Instead I gave him a 16 letter and number code. My Nest thermostat password.

"Turn it up," I said.

"How much?"

"All the way," I said. "I want them feeling like they entered Hell."

"Leave it to me. Do you want it recorded?"

"Yes please," I said.

9 – The Game

In every situation that spirals beyond its expected scope there is a moment, beforehand when things could have been stopped. Everything that happened afterwards can be traced back to the decisions made at a particular point in time which become the catalyst for everything else.

You know the Miracle on The Hudson? Captain Chesley Sullenberger, Sully for short, had just 208 seconds to make a decision that could have doomed or saved the flight and everyone on it. He faced a situation he'd never prepared for, could not have prepared for. How did he make that decision?

To hear him speak it sounds easy. He said he'd prepped his whole life for it. He thought about things. He ran scenarios in his head. He thought about what he'd do if the unexpected ever happened. In none of those thoughts, scenarios and practice runs did he visualize a situation like the one he'd found himself in. But he'd prepared.

All those things he'd done, cumulatively, built neural pathways, responses and plans, that'd created mental heuristics inside his head. He accessed them when crunch point arrived and they helped him think faster and better than if he'd never had anything there. So he did the seemingly impossible. And it worked.

Everything is a game in that respect. It is a pattern with a flow. A surge and an ebb. Identify the pattern correctly and you've solved the game.

My whole life I'd been looking at patterns. Solving problems. Running to just keep in the same place. I could, at the point in time, have chosen to go to the Police. Though beyond the people in my flat I had nothing else to go with and charging someone with breaking and entering wasn't going to solve my problem.

I considered the pattern: someone was after me. They'd invested enough to man four black vans and they'd spent enough to track my client to me in the beginning and also get my identity. I didn't know the going rate for all that but my guess is that it isn't cheap. Certainly more than I was being paid. Conceivably the same someone had made my client disappear and his Secret Service escort.

That was major clout that hinted at even more money.

You can't hide money. It has a weight that is felt. It has an effect that is obvious. So the mysterious someone (or someones) who were after me had money. And they wanted what I had: data.

Specifically the data entrusted to me.

Two questions rose just then: were they interested in obtaining the data or stopping me from getting it to its destination? Both?

The answer here was critical, though for me, none of the outcomes it came with appeared to be good. If they wanted the data it was no good to them without encryption and since I was the only one who could decrypt it they needed me as well and they would have to force me to do it.

Of course I am not stupid. I could have done it for them, except when someone goes to those extremes to get something they're unlikely to then be careful with whoever made things hard for them.

If they wanted to stop me from delivering it … well, then things became even trickier. The range of possibilities that presented themselves then became even more unpalatable to me.

There were a few variables here. Things I considered which threw in fresh uncertainties. Since money was no object I could agree to hand everything over, for a fee. I would be happy. No one would be the wiser. But already they were a little exposed.

In acting the way they had, they had shown their hand. Would they, could they then be OK with just paying me off? I didn't know. Had no way of finding out.

I had no way of actually learning just yet where their red lines lay. What they were prepared to do.

So, the only solution to my predicament, perversely lay in me doing what I had actually been paid to do: my job. There was no other option. With the data delivered safely to its destination all this would go away, though I daresay it appears that then there would be a lot of unhappy people to deal with.

This game then had a solution. The solution presented several different strategies, each of which led to a path of action. This is how the world actually works, though maybe not everything is quite as formalized as what I presented.

I decided, there and then, sitting on the bench at Van Nest Park, temporarily safe and watching he world outside the park's black railings go crazy, what my next step would be.

The game was on and though I didn't quite know all the rules, right now, I called the shots and had the advantage of foreknowledge. My hunters didn't know I knew I was being hunted. That gave me a margin of safety that I was going to use.

I took out my phone and called my Watcher.

***

10 – Communication

"Yo," the voice was instantly recognizable.

"Are you changing shift?"

"What?"

"Are you going to hand over to anyone else any time soon?"

He understood what I was asking. "No man. I got your back. It's you and me all the way to the end." He understood, I think, the subtext of what he'd said and corrected it quickly "Until you deliver your package."

"Good. I want you to do something for me."

"Name it,"

"My door lock is on the security system. Leaving I didn't set it up. But the lock can be activated. Inverse the last six digits of my Nest password and you have the code for that."

"Got it."

"I want you to lock them in. Lock the door and freeze the lock."

"Got it."

"Then call the cops."

Silence.

"Report a disturbance at my address. Give them the details. Say you believe there are armed assailants. You heard screams."

"OK,"

"And don't forget to turn up the thermostat,"

"Already done. Things are beginning to look like fun."

"Ok,"

"Tape everything."

"Doing it already."

"I will call back in once I am safe."

"Got it."

I hang up.

***

Here's a truth: allow someone, anyone to play their game and you've lost already. They know all the rules, they call all the shots and they have prepared for every contingency.

All that's left for you to do is provide the losing they expect you to do.

Change the rules of the game and you've got a chance despite the odds. The trick lies in how you communicate that to the person you're playing the game with. It needs to be done with subtlety and confidence. It has to be done in a way that rocks their own confidence and causes them to reconsider.

Mike Tyson put this more succinctly when he said about boxing that "Everybody has plans until they get hit."

This, then, was my hitting back. And I knew it was going to change their plan.

***

At the corner of Van Nest Avenue and White Plains Road is Islam Fashion. I'd passed it maybe a thousand times over the years without ever giving it much of a thought.

Abaya Lady's Wear Mens Girls & Boys Wear the sign reads, not a comma or apostrophe anywhere. There's a phone number underneath, in case you need to book an appointment maybe?

The window display is colorful. Addressed to women as you'd expect. I timed the vans and left the park with a full twenty minute window. I had to be quick.

There was a strong, unidentifiable to me scent inside. A lady in full Islamic dress minus the veil was behind the counter,

67

arranging a stand-up steamer used to, I guess, iron out the wrinkles from clothes. I was not their target customer.

"May we help you?" she asked. If she looked surprised by my being there she hid it well. I caught sight of an older gentleman unpacking some boxes in the back.

"I'd like to buy a shirt," I said. "Something neutral," I turned towards one of the racks of what looked like men's clothing. There was one long row of the long, traditional Islamic tunics, all different styles and colors. But next to them was an equally long row of cotton shirts. They were a little long, but perfect for my taste.

I chose one, trying it on by holding it in front of the mirror for size. It was short sleeved with alternating thick and thin vertical stripes, all in different shades of either white or orange.

Neatly folded, in stacks, next to them were loose fitting cotton trousers. The sort that traditionally are worn under the tunic. I choose a pair. Checked the waistband for size by holding it up against my hips.

The woman watched me carefully as I did all that.

"Is it for you?" she asked.

I nodded quickly. "Can I try these on?" I said. I knew the answer to that already. It was evident they didn't. "Look," I explained, "I need to change clothes. I will pay for these now," the man in the back looked up and saw me.

Maybe it was my tone of voice or something that caught his attention. Sometimes you can't tell what does it.

"You want to change clothes?" he asked.

I nodded quickly. Checked my watch, I had thirteen minutes left before the vans arrived in their circuit search.

"This way," he motioned me towards a section of the shop in the back. There was a railing on wheels and he quickly threw up an impromptu screen by draping a blue sheet of material over it.

I stepped behind and quickly started undressing.

It is only when you take your clothes off that you realize just how much of who you are is invested in what you wear. The loose-fitting trousers felt flimsy. Insubstantial, like I'd gone from being a knight in armor to fighting barefoot. The shirt equally so. What was an issue however was the sheer lack of pockets. I had nowhere to put my stuff. And the shoes.

I glanced down at my footwear. The man in the mirror in front of me was lanky. The arms thin. The body straight. The loose-fitting trousers called *serwal*, the man had said, made him look reasonably like a Muslim. From a distance. The footwear however was a dead giveaway.

The man was watching me carefully. Gauging what I was thinking. He too followed my gaze to my steel toe-cap, slick black boots. Caterpillars.

Without a word he turned his back to me, went to a cupboard somewhere and I could see him rummaging. He came back with a pair of sneakers. Old, and badly scuffed with stains on one of the laces. But, suddenly, in total character with my outfit. The fit was a little loose, maybe half a size bigger than my usual size but it didn't matter. This, now made me invisible.

He gave me a satchel, made of cloth, to put over my shoulder. In it I placed my wallet, phone and keys. I always travelled light.

"Perfect," I said. I paid for everything in cash. "You can keep my clothes," I motioned with my head to the pile of black I'd been wearing. The man nodded in turn. I wondered, briefly, just what he and the woman might have been thinking but this is Manhattan. Everything is transactional.

I thanked them. Stepped outside and checked my watch.

I'd been in there for nineteen minutes in total. That gave me a full minute. I pulled the satchel so that the strap was worn across my chest, from left to right. It hang snugly at my waist on the right.

I slouched a little, rounding my shoulders to give me a slightly bent over look. Slowed down my step. I tried to think in character. What would a young Muslim be doing out at this time in the Bronx? I made myself feel purposeful but carefree.

A couple of people passed me going the other way and they barely glanced at me. It gave me a sense of confidence in my new look. Then, on cue, the first unmarked black van passed me by. The tinted windows hinted of shadow forms inside. The one on the passenger side, I thought, was staring straight at me. I forced myself to look relaxed.

The van passed. Exactly four minutes later the second one passed me by.

I was in the wind. For now.

It was getting a little darker. I needed a few minutes to formulate my plan and the park was, again, the perfect place to be at.

I crossed the street and entered through the same gate as before. Chose the same bench to sit on. There were a couple of people there this time, not far from me. They barely looked at me.

My fingers dialed the Watchers as I scanned the streets around me, through the park railings.

"Yo,"

"You have a video for me?"

"Hah! Man have I ever?"

"Good, shoot it to my phone."

"Ok,"

I got a ping seconds later. A message with a URL. I clicked on it.

The familiar inside of my apartment felt strange on the small screen. Watching the three men in suits hanging inside my apartment gave it a sense of unreality. That was my place. Wendy's and mine.

It wasn't built for many adults to hang around inside. The Watchers had locked the door and, I suspected, the windows. The thermostat was going up, slowly. And it was hot outside.

It's like watching mice in a lab. The temperature begins to rise. At first the occupants become discomfited. I see how they look at their watches. Check their phones. Fidget. Then they begin to look at each other. Stealing glances at first.

Eventually they begin to talk.

I plugged my earbuds in the phone socket and watched.

"Hey can you turn the AC on or something? It's getting hot in here." From suit one to the other two.

Suit two, closest to the thermostat controls goes there and tries to fiddle with them. Nothing.

It takes another ten minutes of heating to make them realize that it continues to get hotter inside the apartment. They tell each other to open a window. The one by the thermostat continues to fiddle with it, in vain.

Then one of them goes to the window. Tries to open it. The windows are double-glazed. Locked. He panics. Yells.

Panic is contagious. It happens incrementally. At first it raises alarm. Apprehension. Your pulse rate goes up. Then fear begins to rise. You sweat (and they're sweating already). Your hands go clammy. Your pulse rate rises. You can't breathe well.

You shout. Gesticulate. Are quick to apportion blame.

What is most interesting however is what goes on inside your brain. Panic is an emotional response that's activated by specific hormonal secretions in the brain and body. They have direct physiological effects one of which shuts down the higher brain functions you need to coolly appraise a situation.

Decision making, executive decision making requires higher-level networks involved in making decisions. Once they become inaccessible the body goes into pure reaction mode. "Blind panic" is called blind for a reason. It literally blinds you to what is in front of you.

They were not there yet, but they were panicking. There is something terrifying in seeing your fellow, competent agents become helpless and frightened.

They yelled instructions at each other but because they spoke over the top and almost an once, no one was listening.

One grabbed a chair and swung it at the window. It bounced back, once it hit the glass. Double-glazing is notoriously tough. Another raced to the door. It too was locked.

"We're trapped!" He yelled back and that's when panic began to completely take over. They looked around for something sturdier to use as a tool.

As I said, it was a small apartment.

Eventually one of them realized what he'd have to do. He pulled out his gun and fired several shots at the window, the base where the pane met the frame. The double-glazing almost exploded at the impact, the shards of glass flying outwards, hurtling towards the street below. And that's when I heard the police sirens and shouts coming from below. The exchange of looks of pure madness, almost, as the men realized they'd been trapped.

One of them tried to stick his head out the window but a shot rang out and he hastily pulled back. A gas canister came flying in, the smoke obscuring my vision of the events unfolding.

The door appeared to implode. Probably because of a battering ram and then there were more shots, voices, yelling. Lots and lots of screaming. The police were terrified too. And they had more guns.

"One dead. One wounded. Two in custody." The Watcher said when I called him. "The wounded one is at Bronx Lebanon. The other one in custody. Chatter says they're going to be released. Well, not the dead one obviously. But he too will probably go away. Disappear."

"G-men?"

"I don't know yet, though yeah. Some outfit somewhere. They all had some clearance of some kind. The police have some explaining to do it seems."

"Ok. I am going to need some hardware so I will be making a small detour."

"Ok," he was non-committal.

"It's on my way so it won't impact your day. Going down to the Hudson Yards. I know someone there who can hook me up so,"

"Ok,"

"I need a couple of things off you meanwhile,"

"Ask,"

"Tribeca 10007. Apartment 409. Find out who it belongs to. Identify the creeps that broke into my apartment. Tell me who I am dealing with."

"Anything else?"

"For now, no."

I hang up. I needed to handle this. We had to communicate in order to settle it. I'd just sent a strong message back to whoever was after me.

11 – Attack Lines

I am walking. And I am thinking. And thinking is always easier when I am walking. Whenever code gave me a problem I couldn't solve, I'd walk it out.

Neuroscience, these days, is a wand that opens up all sorts of possibilities by providing clear, physical evidence to back up intuitive past beliefs. For example, researchers at New Mexico Highlands University discovered that the foot's impact during walking sends pressure waves through the arteries that significantly modify and can increase the supply of blood to the brain.

As they wrote in their research paper: *"There is a continuum of hemodynamic effects on human brain blood flow within pedaling, walking and running. Speculatively, these activities may optimize brain perfusion, function, and overall sense of wellbeing during exercise."*

It's great to finally have science verify what I'd always maintained. Satchel securely over my shoulder and across my chest. The Harlem River and Third Avenue Bridge were about seven and a half kilometers away, barely four and a half miles. In that distance, in my new get up, I was a needle in a very, very large haystack.

To find me they'd need to have some means of tracking me. At the corner of Van Nest Avenue and Unionport Road was Jay and Jay Grocery Corporation. A corner Grocery store that was literary on a corner, covering both roads, though its address on Google Maps (should anyone care to look) was 1700 Unionport Road.

The guy behind the counter was young and super-friendly. Wendy had bought a pair of unbranded sunglasses once from there. Trying them on in the small mirror tile above the display with the stupid label with the price tag hanging over her nose.

"Do they make me look smart?" she'd teased me.

"Super sophisticated," I'd grinned back. "Definitely have to have them."

They'd cost ten bucks and the store had stuck in my mind ever since. This was the second time I'd visited it. The first since the swatting incident. I don't know if the guy behind the counter recognized me but he flashed me a smile and didn't even blink about my outfit.

That totally determined me to give him a tip. "You have any bandanas?" I asked and he pointed to the back where a display of anklets and bandanas made up their special summer offers. I went through the pretense of choice and choosing my heart clenching in my chest with a physical ache that almost made my knees buckle.

I swear I was almost ready to give it all up there and then. The effort of being me. The effort of doing what I did. The sheer effort of breathing; waking up and staying alive was crushing me.

It occurred to me just how easy it would be to make it all stop. To make it all end. A phone call to my Watchers. The instruction to find those hunting me now, tell them where I was. It would have all been done anonymously. A message sent from a secure server somewhere in Northern France to an exchange in the U.S. where it would then be routed to them.

I imagined the screech of tires. The black, unmarked vans pulling up outside. I couldn't quite visualize the men who'd come out from them but I guessed they wouldn't look much different than the clean-shaven, black suited men who'd broken into my apartment and had waited for me to return, perhaps.

Then, what would happen to me then?

A tag on the elbow. Another, firmer touch on the shoulder as they expertly hemmed me in. Guided me outside, to their waiting vans, ready for any eventuality from me.

They'd want me alive, of course. After all I had the key to the cipher. But there would be no restrictions on hurting me a little. Just so I cooperated.

Pain always makes us react. It's a powerful stimulus. Amoebas, remember?

So, they'd put me in one of their vans. Probably shoot me up with something to soften me. Then? Rendition? Some Black Site somewhere? Until when?

Uncertainties.

Without data we always imagine the worst. And fear, just like pain, makes us react. So, we end up controlling nothing we value. Not ourselves. Not our decisions. Not our world.

If you want to know the truth the Earth will be inherited by the fearless. Except those who display that kind of pathology will, by definition, have short, glorious lives.

Pain also makes us feel alive.

Depends how you see it. Descartes thought it was all about thinking and chose to define existence that way. But really it is all about feeling because, you guessed it, there is not a whole lot of thinking going on. By any of us.

The thought made me angry and anger can be a useful emotion. Especially when you're on the run. "Face paint, you have any crayons?" I asked and the guy behind the counter obligingly pointed me in the right direction.

I paid in cash.

Thus, with a bandana round my neck, hiding the lower part of my face, despite the warmth of the day and crayon lines applied in skin tone across my face I was confident that face recognition software would fail to pick me up.

Walking cleared my head. My breathing became even. Deep. A message sent to an adversary in order to establish communication is lost if there's no opportunity for them to talk to you.

It's logical. In the absence of information the other party misunderstands your actions. Fails to grasp your motives.

What happens then is escalation. When we're afraid we over-compensate.

I knew whoever was after me had means. Both in terms of money and resources.

I called my Watcher.

"Yo,"

"Anything?"

"Yeah. Interesting stuff. The dudes in your apartment are ex-secret Service. Been retired for over two years. Probably working private. Or at least off the books."

"All three?"

"Yeah. Their IDs checked out. They all have a file."

"I'm sorry about the dead one."

"Don't be. I ran their prints off the Police server. I don't know if the police know this yet but there are few unsolved homicides that have their signature."

"They're hit men?" I was a little incredulous. Certainly they hadn't looked like stone-cold killers on the video. Then again what did stone-cold killers were supposed to look like? My little stunt had caught them by surprise.

"There's more."

"OK," my mind was racing.

"I picked up a scrambled communiqué. Inter-service. I was running a routine scan to see if I can pick up any useful chatter concerning you."

"And?"

"Looks like your client's detail showed up on the shores of the Hudson,"

I digested that.

"Dead?"

"Looks like an accident but … you believe that you should be writing a letter to Santa extolling your good behavior this year,"

I couldn't help but smile. Was my client dead? If so it raised other possibilities. The obvious, practical ones here were about money as in I needed to get paid at the end of my job. For that I needed to have a client. Preferably a live one.

"My client?"

"Not amongst the listed dead," he managed to stress the word "listed" by raising the inflexion of his voice.

"OK," an unknown. One more unknown factor to add here.

"Have you got any good news to give me?"

"You're still alive and well, aren't you?"

He had a point. "Barely,"

He chortled. "I will keep you that way."

"The Tribeca address?"

"That's proving surprisingly difficult," he said. "Not because it's hidden, but because it's not. The apartment is registered to a Cayman Island Corporation. Bought last year for thirty eight million dollars. I mean, who has that kind of money for an apartment that you won't even use?" he asked. It was an academic question.

He went on: "The Corporation is part of a chain. Some trust from London owns majority shares. Then there is an investment vehicle that constitutes the bulk of the trust. Each of these is transparent as you can guess, but the moment you look deeper everything disappears. The trail leads to somewhere else."

"How far have you got?"

"New York. Stock Exchange. There's a brokerage that parks some of its funds in a temporary holding account. Then ships them out to transact trades on behalf of its clients. That temporary account is never empty and the core sum of it that is seemingly never touched despite all the transactions is thirty eight million dollars. Sounds familiar?"

"Why that number? Why not keep more? Or even, less?"

"My guess. The sum is a guarantee of some kind. It's linked to the apartment. I don't yet know the connections."

"Keep digging,"

"That I will."

"One more thing."

"Of course,"

"I want to talk to those who're hunting me."

"What?"

"Com'on you've got to stop being surprised by my requests. After all you're an analyst. You know how this is playing out."

Long pause. Then: "We don't get many situations like yours. It's beginning to feel challenging."

"I know. Same this end. This is why I need to talk to them. Can you set up a front number? Something we can burn?"

"Of course. I need half an hour. Maybe forty minutes for something untraceable."

"Ok, do it please. Then get the number to them."

"I have one of the G-man's cell. The one from your apartment."

"Great. Use him. I want to talk to his boss."

"And?"

"I want you to trace it all. They will try and track me. No one stays invisible."

"OK,"

"And send them the video."

"Send it to whom?"

"Hmmm," I thought for a minute. I needed to make a splash. "Can you send it to the News Network?"

"NNC?"

"Yes. They will most probably be reporting on the incident. Strip the sound. Send only visual. That way it will be all the more compelling."

"Smart. Ok. Will do."

He hang up.

Mentally, as I walked, I played out all the points. What we'd discussed. It was all falling into some kind of order. A picture was beginning to emerge, I just couldn't quite grasp it yet. Couldn't understand its shape.

"It's war," I thought. Someone had enough clout to arrange for the expert detail of my client to have an 'accident'. I really didn't like that fuck but wishing him dead was maybe a little too far. Plus, he owed me twenty thousand.

It was time to speak to Slater.

12 – Slater

Networks. Each person in it is a node. A single point of data. Edges. These are the connective threads that join each person to someone or something else.

Edges are made up of interest. Attention. Engagement. It takes effort to maintain them which means that there has to be some motivation. Motivation is supplied by self-interest. If all this sounds a little bit transactional, you're right, it is.

It takes effort to maintain any connection. That effort, in turn, is justified because it feeds into our sense of self, identity, career aims, security … the list goes on.

Do we think in this transactional, coldly calculating way? No, we don't. We think in terms of feelings. Emotions like happiness, jealousy, fear, envy.

They make us do the things we do.

Slater. I knew Slater from law school days. On and off. We crossed paths professionally. He was rich. Well, richer than me. He won cases more than I did. He had rich clients.

I struggled.

I quit.

He carried on. Became Mr Big.

Well, he became the highly paid concierge of specific services: sensitive legal advice, which is a euphemism on how to break the law. Purveyor of exotic services, like yours truly. C'est moi.

Slater was methodical. He kept track of information. Knew how to keep data so that it didn't lose its value. And Slater had brought me a client who may or may not be dead.

If nothing else I needed to know what would happen to the rest of my money. At the Hudson Yards I had a contact. Someone I could rely on to deliver any kind of help I might need. There was a price involved, of course. Everything is transactional. That's what gives it value. But the price wasn't always money.

I made a call to my Watcher.

"Yo,"

"Can you connect me to Slater?"

"The go-between?"

It was an odd, archaic term that I found amusing but yeah, I guess that's what Slater really was. "Yeah. His number is on my cloud-based archive. The password-"

"Got it." He cut me off.

I thought for a brief moment. I hadn't given him the password to that. He knew that.

"How?"

"When you were made. I hacked into your cloud accounts. Checked to see you weren't being cleaned out."

"Ok. And?"

"You data is safe. I threw an additional VPN around everything."

I hesitated for a moment. Then: "Thank you."

"It's what we do. I got Slater."

My phone rang. I picked up on the second ring. "Slater,"

"What the hell is going on Alex?" he was yelling down the line.

"I may as well ask you that. You sent goons at my place to wait for me?" I knew he hadn't, but I was fishing.

"Of course not. Why the heck would I do that? My client, our client has disappeared."

"I know. Someone's after me."

"The data?"

"Safe with me. For now," I added that last part as a veiled threat.

"Alex, that data must remain safe."

"As long as I get paid it will."

"Alex you need to deliver it."

"I need to do nothing until I know that I am getting paid."

"Relax, relax. You will get paid."

"Another twenty thousand as agreed."

"Yes, of course. As agreed."

"And whose after me now?"

"I don't know Alex. I swear."

He was lying. I could almost hear it in his voice.

"OK, Slater," I said, "later."

"Alex wait – "

I hang up. If he'd tried to call me back he'd get a dead connection. The number I'd appeared to call from was now dead.

The phone rang again. I picked up as I walked. "Yeah,"

"Slater was trying to trace you," said my Watcher.

"Interesting. Did he get far?"

"Yes. Pretty good equipment. State-issue, for sure."

"Ok, thanks."

Metadata. Everything reveals something. It is inescapable. State-issue equipment doesn't come cheap. State-sponsored actors mean that more than money was at stake.

***

"You know Alex, sometimes I just don't know how far we will get," Wendy had said that to me eighteen months ago. Precisely.

I was caught up checking something. I nodded, half listening to her. She was sprawling on the one sofa we had in the middle of our apartment. In her underwear, looking at the ceiling. It was a Sunday and I was working when I shouldn't.

Wendy in her underwear was always a distraction. Her body made me feel good, deep inside. The way it contoured. The swell of her breasts just above her bra. The panties she wore that were always cut high on the side and showed off her legs to perfection.

"What'd you mean?" I said eventually.

She was lying on her back, looking up at the ceiling and playing with her hair. "Oh, nothing."

"Com'on," I smiled at her, half getting out of my chair.

"No, stay," she stopped me. "Finish off what you're doing."

I had.

I shouldn't have.

I should have just gone over and kissed her. Told her how much she meant to me. How –

How.

Fuck!

Fuck!

Fuck!

I felt the emptiness begin inside and wondered to myself whether I was done. Whether I had been done for some time but simply didn't know that yet.

I will tell you something I've only thought about since I lost her. The basic building block of civilization is a dyad. Two people. Acting as a single node. Because a dyad is a publicly acknowledge union that usually consists of publicly exchanging marriage vows or somehow formalizing a relationship everything revolves around that.

Two people nest. They feed. They multiply. They need furniture stores and convenience stores and hospitals and courts and an army. They need a nation that needs a government that creates boundaries and borders.

Everything you can think of has really happened because of the tension that exists in a union between two individuals who experience internal feelings that they try to satisfy through external events.

Shopping. Entertainment. Education. Religion. Fashion. Civilization. Look at every film you see and it is basically a love story gone wrong.

The U.S. Marines have a say: "Two is one. One is none." It signifies teamwork. The fact that no soldier can truly stand alone for very long and survive.

I am none.

13 – Route

Everything happens for a reason. No, I am not going all metaphysical and gooey on you right now. I am more of a cause and effect guy. Nothing happens without some cause and when it happens it has an effect. It's just sometimes both cause and effect are so far removed from each other that when the particular something that should be connected to them, happens. It's not easy to see the chain of events.

Walking clears the mind. Intuitively you know that. But you most probably don't know why that happens. Sure, you can make all sorts of educated guesses: change of environment, removal of distractions, isolation from aggravation, the opportunity to finally be alone with one's thoughts. All of these.

Neuroscience will agree that walking helps clear the mind and focus your thinking but neuroscientists will also tell you that al the intuitive reasons you ascribe to this are patently false.

I spend a lot of time online. I look at studies and I read reports. I email scientists and I engage in deep thought. Without Wendy I have a lot of free time, which is why I know that *"brain blood flow is very dynamic and depends directly on cyclic aortic pressures that interact with retrograde pressure pulses from foot impacts. There is a continuum of hemodynamic effects on human brain blood flow within pedaling, walking and running. Speculatively, these activities may optimize brain perfusion, function, and overall sense of wellbeing during exercise."*

In other words the impact of the foot on the ground when you walk changes the blood flow to the brain and synchs with the beating of the heart. Walking (and running) we feel the most alive we've ever been. But most importantly we become smarter.

Pretty sure this is not something that happens when you travel around in blacked out vans with tinted windows.

I dialed my Watcher.

"Yo,"

"You have a name?"

He hesitated. I said: "It's going to be an interesting night. Maybe I should call you something."

"No names," he said.

"You know mine."

"You're the client."

Fair enough. "Get Slater back," I said.

"Give me one mo,"

As good as his word. A moment later.

"Alex?" Slater's voice sounded panicked. "What have you done Alex?" He must have got wind of the stiff, the two who got arrested.

"Who's after me?"

"Alex, I told you already, I don't know."

"No, what you said was that you wanted me to think you didn't know. I thought you knew me better than that."

"Alex this is no game."

"You're damn fucking right it isn't. Who's after me?"

"Don't know. I don't know names. Government for sure. FBI maybe, Homeland. They have a lot of clout."

"You have a point man?"

He hesitated.

"Slater, I still have the data," I reminded him.

"Yes. Alright. I have a point man. You're gonna deliver the data?"

"That's the deal. Give me his name."

"Col. Adams."

"Adams?" Had I heard that name before? I was straining to remember but nothing was coming up. "OK, Slater." I said.

"What are you going to do?"

"As promised, deliver your data. Get paid." I know that didn't make a lot of sense given the context of my situation but sometimes people under stress just want to hear that things, somehow, magically will get back to normal. Slater was no different.

"OK, Alex. OK. Do that. Exactly. Do as you've agreed. But before you do so we have to meet."

"Why?"

"There are things I can't say right now. Things you need to know."

Deviations from the norm have a reason. That reason is not usually good. That's why we have a norm. I mean, if we were all to agree that killing is a pretty bad thing to do and we need really strict laws to prevent it and punish any transgressor, it would make zero sense to add in the caveat that it's maybe OK to kill on Fridays. Or on a really, really rainy day.

That would make no sense at all.

"You know the Marcus Garvey Park? Harlem 125th Street?"

"Yeah."

"Meet me there in an hour."

"An hour. OK, Alex. Marcus Garvey Park."

"How shall I reach you if I need to?"

"You can't." I hang up. Not only was Slater lying but he was, my guess, playing both ends against the middle. And the middle, in this case, was me.

I called my Watcher.

"Yo,"

"Traced again?"

"Yes. He came close but I threw up extra screen layers this time, anticipating this. But there is someone else too."

"What do you mean?"

"The damnedest thing. When Slater started tracing you, I could see the tracking software. One part of it originates in Langley,"

"The C.I.A? They're spooks. They have zero homegrown jurisdiction."

"Yeah. That's just it. They came on afterwards. Slater's friends are local boys. My guess is a heavy duty van in NYC somewhere. Some pretty powerful telemetry on it."

"Homeland,"

"Most likely. The Langley group however, I don't know. They took some pretty serious steps to hide themselves from the Homeland guys."

"Interesting."

"Totally weird. What do you want me to do?"

"Find out the identity of the Tribeca 10007 apartment. That's vital. Call me when you do."

"And you?"

"I am going to try and make my appointment with Slater." I said.

Cause and effect. My steps were taking me closer and closer to that moment in the Docks when my brain was about to be splattered outside my head and everything that made me, Alex, was going to vanish forever.

At least, I thought, I was seeing straight. My Cooper's Color Code was now active and the color was red. Deep, deep, red.

14 – Made

You never quite realize what alone means until you find yourself in New York City, getting dark, unable to go home. Unable to walk openly. Feeling that you're the target of some giant malevolent machine that is out to crash you.

Walking, alone, head hunched defensively in my shoulders. Head down. Gait shortened just in case they were using advanced analytics to pick me out from the crowd.

You notice things when you walk. And the things you notice can sometimes destroy you.

Wrapped in my thoughts. Dressed in my isolation. I saw couples walking hand-in-hand. A girl reaching up on tip toe to kiss the man she was with. Couples in cars. Warm lights beginning to light up residences and apartments.

Inside, I imagined, lives were being played out exactly as they should. Some couples would have sex. Others would quarrel and make up. And others still would sit quietly, making plans about dinner and thinking out the rest of their lives.

Of course I know, and you know, and I know you know that it doesn't quite work like that. But complexities aside. Personal difficulties notwithstanding. Every time we find ourselves in that situation where we walk alone, apart from the crowd, the one thing we really want to have again is that connection.

We want to find that someone special. We want to share moments with someone who isn't us. We want to feel that the "one" we feel is the "one" the U.S. Marines talk about where two make up a single, indivisible, totally in synch and therefore formidable, unit.

For a while. Wendy and I were that unit. She was my anchor. The person who made me feel whole. Somewhere along the line I forgot to tell her that. And what she knew she forgot because memories are built to degrade.

What do amoebas do when they experience pain because of something in their path? They move in the opposite direction and away from it.

The pain of my thoughts made stop thinking so deeply. I had no choice but to be where I was, heading for where I was heading. Remember what I said about Free Will? It is the cruelest of illusions because the moment you think you have it is the moment when you realize you never did.

***

"You don't appreciate me any more." It's the kind of accusation you have no way of fighting against. Deny it and you sound defensive. Ignore it and you prove it correct. Try to provide examples that refute it and you sound petulant. Ask for examples to support it and you become combative.

When Wendy said that to me I was getting ready to go on a data run. Nothing big. Maybe a few hours of work all told. I needed to head to Queens.

"Can we talk about this later?" was the best I could manage. I told myself that I'd use the run to think things through, try to understand what was happening to us. How we could fix it.

Were my feelings the same? I tried to honestly answer that one and every time I tried I became convinced that it was a hopeless task that would only lead me into a deeper and more dangerous trap.

A word of advice: the moment you start thinking about your relationship in terms of tactics and strategy and traps is the time to get out.

I should have given that advice to myself, there and then. I didn't. Instead I opted to work as if nothing was amiss and everything was OK.

It wasn't.

***

I'm not sure when I became uneasy. As I walked I'd noticed something but I wasn't sure what. That made me go on alert and pay attention. Attention is like a directional beacon. It lights up what you're looking at so you can see it properly. Once you see it you can assess it.

A grey Audi went by as I walked. Two male occupants inside. There was a stiffness about the way they were sat like they were focused on looking only ahead. Just like the difference between erotic art and just plain porn you know it only when you see it. There was an unnaturalness in the way they sat, their demographic, that triggered alarms in me.

Of course trying to track a guy on foot in a car is never very smart. Caught up in traffic the Audi went ahead and presently disappeared in the traffic. I thought that if they were tracking me they'd have to find a way to turn around again, try and pick me up. I scanned my memory to see if the Audi had been in traffic before.

I vaguely remembered something but I couldn't be sure I wasn't manufacturing it. Conjuring up mirages to satisfy my paranoia. Wendy would have loved that. She did say I was becoming paranoid. Right there, near the end.

"Alex, that's just plain stupid," she'd say. "You're getting paranoid."

It wasn't. I wasn't.

I was approaching Clark Playground on 357 E and 144th Street. I was going to get off the road. And, I thought, I really need to do something about a change of clothes. It occurred to me that I hadn't perhaps brought enough cash with me for this

92

data run. It was beginning to look way more challenging than any data run I'd ever done before.

***

I had placed a hidden app on Wendy's phone. A new GPS tracker on her laptop bag. And another app in her laptop. I was taking no chances. The triangulation of the data. Its convergence; told a revealing story.

"I told you I went out with the girls," Wendy said. The girls were her group of friends. Occasionally they'd get together and just blow off steam.

Except I knew that she hadn't. and she was lying.

Not OK.

And I chose to accept it because I wasn't yet sure what to do.

You see, the road to hell is no longer made up of good intentions. That road is paved by intent and misalignment of values. It is made slippery with fear and uncertainty. It is made possible with pain.

I slid down that path.

I am in my own personal purgatory.

***

"Yo,"

I dialed in. "I have company."

"You sure?"

"No. But I think I do."

"Wait,"

I did.

"No. You're clean,"

"Are you certain?"

"You're in the park?"

"No, the playground,"

"Same diff,"

93

"OK,"

"Cameras at the intersection and also on the street corner across from you. I scanned the area. All's good. No one followed you. No one saw you enter and paid attention."

"You're sure?"

"Yes- " The voice was abruptly cut off. There was the sudden screech of tires, coming from two sides. Two black vans appeared virtually out of nowhere.

I didn't wait to see who was coming out of them. Fear made me jump off one of the swings I'd been sitting on and scramble to the far side on hands and knees, keeping low and putting the slide between whoever was coming and me.

My heart was racing. My mind was on fire.

Suits.

I almost relaxed there and then. But something made me stay low. They entered the playground in pairs and I almost admired the military precision with which they'd implemented the U.S. Marine's basic dictum. "Two is one."

They held guns in front of them. Pistols. Flat, sleek, black and menacing looking. They stood one slightly behind each other and they divided the area in front of them in half, pistols held in the classic two-handed grip pioneered and formalized by what should now be a familiar name to you: Lieutenant Colonel Jeff Cooper. Yep, the same man who gave us the Cooper Color Code and mine was now flashing on red again.

They entered the playground expertly quartering the area with their eyes. Pistols held at eye level so they could use the sights.

I was cut off from my Watchers. I tried, calling them. The call went dead even as I dialed so the area was being cordoned off. Clever. Scary. Powerful stuff.

I wouldn't be the only one affected though my guess was that it was a really tight range they were using to block my calls so not that many people would be affected and certainly they could, unlike me, just walk out of the affected area.

There were two, four, six of them in total, walking in slowly, almost back to back they way they were grouped and positioned, knees bent for stability, eyes scanning. It was beautiful to watch. Terrifying too. Instinct told me to keep still. Fear froze me where I was. That, probably saved my life.

It took them seconds longer to spot me in the diminishing light conditions. They'd come in some way into the playground then. Were fanning out.

One saw me. Instinctively he straightened out his arms. The gun in front of him coughed. Something pinged hard inches above my head, hitting the rail of the slide and sending sparks flying with a strong metallic noise.

I was scrambling. On hands and knees. Moving as fast as I could. A sound of terror escaping my lips. My right show snugged on something on the ground. In mad panic I pulled, thrashed. Slipped. More muted coughs from the guns held by the men in suits. Bullets flew over my head as I lay on the ground, momentarily flat. I cried out. A guttural, atavistic sound. And my last coherent thought was that Wendy would appreciate the irony of my situation. Completely.

I didn't hear the muted coughs that came after that. I felt them though. The air vibrated. There was the thud of bullets impacting flesh. The guttural push of air being violently shoved out of lungs as pieces of metal punch their way through flesh.

A bullet is a marvelous, crazy thing. It's tiny. It pierces flesh making a wound and uses its momentum to carve out a path through it.

There are one of two ways it can kill you: One, it destroys something vital your body needs to stay alive. You then begin to bleed and go into shock. Shock occurs when a person loses blood flow to his or her organs. This lack of blood flow depletes one's organs of much-needed oxygen and requires emergency medical attention. If you don't get it, you're most likely dead.

Two, the bullet creates a massive channel that damages flesh in its path. The term ballistics refers to in the science of the travel of a projectile in flight is cavitation. A "permanent" cavity is caused by the path of the bullet itself with crushing of tissue, whereas a "temporary" cavity is formed by radial stretching around the bullet track from continued acceleration of the medium (air or tissue) in the wake of the bullet, causing the wound cavity to be stretched outward. For projectiles traveling at low velocity the permanent and temporary cavities are nearly the same, but at high velocity and with bullet yaw the temporary cavity becomes larger.

Death is a fascinating outcome not because it happens at all but because there are so many ways to get you there and so many of them are man-made. The man-made ones have complexities and, sometimes, unforeseen consequences. The natural one, of course, is imposed by the physical laws of the universe. Namely, the second law of thermodynamics that states that even when work is done to impose order, disorder is the natural, inevitable and remorseless state of the universe. At some point you simply have no available energy to impose order upon the collection of atoms and molecules that constitute your body and it degrades.

You die.

All this went through my head as I heard more than felt the deadly thud of metal biting flesh and considered what I knew of the mathematics of wound ballistics.

I lay there a few moments more. On the ground. Flat on my stomach. My arms covering my head in a useless gesture of protection. My body in shock. My breathing rugged. Gasps. My throat clenched in fear and suppressed agony. Thinking that I was dying.

"You OK?" It was a voice I didn't recognize. It had a distinct Brooklyn twang to it. I peeked over my elbow.

Two guys in jeans and polo shirts stood over me, looking down. What caught my attention were the long, round thickly silenced barrels of the semi-automatics they held at their sides. The barrels were smoking.

My gaze dropped level to the ground again. At ground level I had a worm's eye view of the scene on the playground, past the feet of the two men who stood over me.

On the ground, splayed like an artful arrangement of a human origami flower, were the bodies of the six men in suits who'd come after me. I'd heard the thuds and I'd felt the thrumming vibration in the air as bullets had flown at me, over me.

One, I saw, had his eyes open. A look of frozen surprise in them.

"They're dead?" I asked and I could hear both the senselessness of my question and the croak in my voice as I struggled to make a meaningful conversational sound. I remembered the wailing I'd thought I'd heard as I had scrambled for my life. The crazy sound that'd come out of my throat.

My voice was not quite my own just yet.

"We had to wait for them to come into the playground," the man standing above me said. "I'm sorry, but taking them out sooner wouldn't guarantee we'd get them and there were more of them than us."

"Who are you?" I croaked.

And the earbud in my ear came to life as my Watcher called back: "Alex, are you OK? There are reports of shots fired in your area. Just after you went dark. Cops on the way,"

"We'll explain on the way. Come with us. Cops will be here soon," the man who'd been doing all the talking was around 35 I thought.

"Where are we going?"

"We want you to deliver the data you have to the place you've been contracted to," the phrasing was careful. Each word meant to help me snap out of my fear and focus on my task.

"They're jamming us," I said, my voice still felt very tight. It was an effort to speak. "There must be more of them, around."

"Oh, the guys in the van," said my interlocutor. "I wouldn't worry about them."

It explained why the signal to my phone was back on.

I came up on hands and knees. Placed a finger on my ear to talk to the Watcher. "How far out? The Police?" I asked. My phrasing inelegant because my thoughts were still all over the place. Adrenaline was making me shake, it made it hard to get back on my feet.

"Four minutes out, maybe five. They're going through red lights," he said.

"Ok," I turned to the guys standing over me. One of them, the one who'd done all the talking offered me his hand. I took it. Scrambled to my feet.

"We have some decent clothes for you," he said looking at my outfit. My loose white trousers were ripped at the knees and now looking way less white than before. My shirt was also dirty. "This way," he took hold of my elbow and guided me gently but firmly. I let him.

The other one, all this time, had never let his eyes off the area around us. He kept on scanning the streets, checking to see if someone was coming.

"We need to move," he said. His voice clipped. Also Brooklyn.

"This way," the one holding my elbow steered me. They led me through the playground gate. All this time I secretly marveled at the efficiency of movement that allowed them to carry their semi-autos single-handedly, on their side. The position, with the barrel running along the side of the leg, hid the shape of the weapon and made it it less conspicuous. Yet it didn't hamper ease of movement. It could have been brought up to bear at any time.

Two, just two of them. I felt they looked familiar, like I'd seen them before but my mind brought nothing up.

The one that'd done all the talking and I were in front. He was holding my elbow, still. Firmly. The other one brought up the rear. Eyes scanning everything.

Walking this way we made our way to East 144th Street side of the playground. One of the lampposts, about fifty yards away had been disabled. In its deeper shadow was parked a black, unmarked van.

"They have all sorts of gear in it," said the one who was steering me by the elbow. "I destroyed it of course, but they'll get more. Funding is not a problem for them in this,"

I looked at him with a half-dazed expression on my face.

"This way," he steered me again, fingers digging deep into my elbow. His grip felt like a vice. My legs numbly complied and I turned towards where he was pointing me towards.

There, on the side of the road, parked in a no-parking zone was a grey Audi.

"That's our ride," said the man holding my elbow and in total synch with his words, the car's lights flashed a momentary 'alarm off' signal and the courtesy light inside came automatically on.

Everything became too much for me at that moment. I doubled up and with a wretch that made me feel like I was spitting out my stomach, I threw up in front of it.

15 – The Ride

Context. To understand how important it is consider that data gives rise to culture. Let me explain this further for you: Everything is data. The things we do. The things we think. The things we think that make us do the things we do. Data is, as W. H. Auden wrote in his poem about love "good morning and good night". He was referring to the law in that line but the analogy is a perfect fit. The law is culture and the perfect example of how data gives rise to culture.

The little things we do. Our good mornings and good nights create patterns of behavior that fall into the usually binary division of acceptable and unacceptable. What is unacceptable to the body social becomes the law that rules against it. Where acceptable rubs at the edge of unacceptable you get the grey zone of interpretation.

That interface is dynamic.

New data gives rise to new culture. Context changes culture. Which then affects data. The #MeToo movement case in point. What used to be acceptable, even if it was unpalatable, has now become unacceptable. What's really changed things however is the context. Women have more power because they work more and have more earning capacity. This changes their sense of self-worth. But that is a trite way of looking at things. What has made the unpalatable unacceptable is transparency.

The network effect that makes everyone who thinks that the unpalatable shouldn't be acceptable creates a momentum that generates the context through which everything is either relevant or not.

Relevance determines value. Context does that which is a way of saying that context creates value in culture.

I was sitting on data that had value. I knew that. But without context its relevance escaped me. The suits tonight and the ones at my apartment weren't after the data, or at least not directly. They were after me.

Me.

In my line of work secrets are taken to the grave. This data had to be kept secret I guess. At all costs. The only way to bury it was to bury the messenger.

None of this presaged anything good for me and these were my thoughts as the two men drove me towards where they said I had to keep my appointment with whoever this data I carried was intended for.

"You have names?" I asked. I was sat in the backseat, looking at the back of their heads and they both turned to look at me sideways when I asked.

They exchanged a glance. Then: "Tomas," the driver said. "He'd been doing most of the talking,"

"Michal," said the other.

Ok. That was a good sign. They didn't intend to kill me and at that point my paranoia was in full swing. "Who do you work for?" I asked.

"Not Homeland," said Tomas.

"Or FeeBees," added Michal.

The car was going exactly the regulation speed for the road. A smooth, easy drive designed to attract zero attention from anyone.

"So, who then?"

"Let's say we're independent contractors," Tomas said. They looked at each other again and smirked at their own inside joke.

I wasn't really going to get a straight answer out of them.

"Do you know where I am going?"

"Tribeca 10007," Michal said.

"Ok. Yeah. I need to make one quick stop."

"No stops," Tomas this time. He was clearly the leader of the two.

"It's important,"

"We drop off the data. You get paid. Then you can go anywhere you like,"

"I am the only one who can decrypt the data," I reminded them. They gave each other that special look.

"We're the ones who're keeping you alive," Tomas said. "We too have orders and they're to take you straight there."

"The stop is on its way," I said. Once we cross Harlem River. Marcus Garvey Park,"

"No way."

"It's about the data," I said. That made them turn and look at me. "Slater has something I need," I explained.

"You're meeting Slater there?"

"Yes, it's important," I stressed.

They did what they'd been doing in front of me: exchanged a look. Then nodded in unison. That's something they hadn't done before.

"OK, we'll take you there," Tomas said and turned his attention to his driving.

"Here, put these on," Michal said. He handed to me a pair of dark cargo pants and a grey Tee. "No shoe change. Sorry."

The white Nike trainers clashed a little now, I thought. The thought made me smile because it was so incongruous. I'd almost died. I hadn't, of course.

Bad luck.

16 – The Meeting

One distinct advantage of riding in a car? Speed. Mobility changed the face of civilization taking the lines of contact and communication from the 3.1 miles per hour which are the average walking speed of a man to the 12 miles per hour which is the trot of a horse.

We've been going faster and faster ever since, riding in vehicles that can take us further, longer.

Viewed like this we are each a node of information. A data point made up of memories, knowledge and experience. The three things that go to create perception. Add enough of us with a similar enough perception in the vicinity of each other, throw in some way of communicating with each other and you have a version of reality that is sufficiently well understood to support civilization.

You see now the value of information. The State was willing to kill me. I was, I thought to myself as I stood on the rock promontory inside the park itself. I was early thanks to the unexpected car ride.

My escort had insisted on coming with me.

"No way are you doing this on your own," Tomas said. "The ones sent to kill you won't have called in and by now a new team will be on its way,"

I shuddered at the matter-of-fact tone he had as he said all this.

I insisted they stayed out of sight. "Slater spooks easily," I said. "He sees me with you he'll think I've sold him out,"

"How do you know he hasn't sold you out?" Tomas asked.

Valid point, I didn't.

"We'll keep an eye out for you," Tomas said. Both he and Michal had checked the magazines in their guns and did that movie thing you see in films where a bullet is chambered in a handgun.

Somehow it didn't make me feel any safer than before.

There is a rocky rise in the park itself. In the dark, with the clothing I wore, I would be relatively inconspicuous. I still had ten minutes to wait before Slater appeared provided he was even on time.

My escort of two had expertly melted in the dark. I strained my eyes to see them but I truly felt I was the only one in the park. I recalled how eerily effective they'd been at hiding in the playground. How deadly they'd been. How casually they were taking all this.

Away from them I used the time. Called my Watcher.

"Yo,"

"You got me?"

"Yep. Been tracking your signal sine the playground. That was some seriously effective block they had. Shut you down like a Faraday cage."

"Yeah, military grade at least. What's the chatter?"

"Dead stiffs in the playground. Police are calling it a gang war."

"Right."

"I've checked the db to see what they truly are. They came up as Homeland Security. Independent contractors. Four of them with tours of duty. Iraq, Afghanistan."

"Shit!"

"Yeah, I know."

"Did you find out who owns apartment 409?"

"Yeah. It wasn't easy. I had to use direct local contacts in Belize and then Estonia. But I got it."

"Well?"

"Well, what?"

"Don't mess with me. What's the name?"

Pause. Then: "Alberto Motisi."

My blood ran cold. I wished I'd misheard. I hoped that my Watcher had made a mistake. I was praying to gods I'd never prayed to before that it was all a horrible mistake, a dream that would evaporate the moment I opened my eyes.

"Are you sure?" I know it's unnecessary but I was thinking on my feet and asking a pointless question allowed me time to think.

"Of course. I checked so as to not make mistakes. It's his. Ultimately."

"Ok, thank you."

"You're welcome. And Alex – "

"Yeah,"

"I am glad you're still alive."

"Heh! Me too. Me too."

***

Some things don't make sense until they do. Manhattan real estate is the most expensive real estate in the world. I should know for what I paid for a tiny cell in the better side of The Bronx.

Slater was part of the puzzle. More accurately he held information that would make the missing pieces of the picture suddenly appear before me.

I sat down on the rocky outcrop and waited, mulling things over in my head.

Betrayal has a familiar feel to it. I should know. Wendy betrayed me in the end. She betrayed us. I then betrayed her. Betrayal, like fear, is contagious. It feeds upon expectations and perceptions and it is triggered by behavior that increases the level of uncertainty.

105

Schrodinger's cat requires uncertainty to exist, equally, between two possible states but it takes trust to maintain at least one of them.

Psychologists will tell you that "Betrayal means "an act of deliberate disloyalty," Betrayal has to do with destroying someone's trust, possibly by lying." Neuroscientists now understand that betrayal assessment really is a trust calculation that involves our understanding of the level of uncertainty that is introduced by someone else's motives.

I was pretty sure that Slater had sold me out. He'd betrayed me, though I also understood the exigencies involved. I felt no rancor. Only sadness because his betrayal triggered memories of mine. Memories of Wendy's betrayal.

"Why so sad?" She'd asked that on that fateful day.

Sometimes words fail.

How can you say "I know." What words can adequately convey knowledge of the loss of trust? "I know you're lying. I know you're no longer mine."

"Work stuff," I mumbled and bent my head in my laptop.

"See you tonight then," she'd said and her voice felt light, airy. Happy?

Was she, really, truly happy? No longer mine, but pretending. No longer with me, but still playing a role? And she, in all the cognitive dissonance she must be feeling, was OK?

What then that made me? Five words that have no answer I can ever grow to like.

Self-reflection is a mine field. You may enter thinking you will find a path out of whatever funk you're feeling but things are more likely to blow up in your face and maim you.

"Alex?"

Slater walked towards me, in the darkness. Arms to the side. He was dressed in slacks and open neck, white short. It made him stand out in the low-level light.

"Over here," I stood up.

He stopped, lowered his hands and then, walked towards me.

"You still have the data?" was the first thing he asked.

"What is going on Slater?"

"You still have it?"

I ignored his question. Stayed where I was, forcing him to come to me. Said: "You knew all this was going to happen you son of a bitch,"

"No Alex. No." he denied it immediately. "I didn't. I-"

"Is the president's son dead?"

Data and metadata. The deadly dance of information and interpretation. Slater was going to give me the context I needed. Most of it. Maybe.

"No. He's safe. His escort is dead, though."

"I heard,"

He processed that. Said: "You have the data?"

"What is it?"

"What?"

"What is that data?"

"Alex, you saw it, same as I did. Some satellite images. I don't know."

"Why is it so important that people are dying?"

"I don't know. I only know who it's going to and why."

"Tell me,"

"The Hudson Yards project."

"Our Hudson Yards project? The Chelsea and Hudson Yards neighborhoods?"

"Yeah. It's the largest private real estate development in the United States by area which might just make it the most expensive real estate development on the planet. You may not really appreciate the size of it but it's twenty five billion dollars."

He let that sink in for effect. I knew I could Google over one hundred countries across the globe whose GDP was below that. I listened intently to his explanation.

"Its development costs have come mainly from Related Companies and Oxford Properties who are the primary developers and major equity partners in the project, alongside some foreign investors through the EB-5 investment program. Mitsui Fudosan is one of the foreign investors. Tucson Estates is another due to where its HQ is at."

Tucson Estates I recalled because it was in the news very recently having to cough up nine hundred million dollars on a loan to stay afloat. That kind of money sticks to mind.

"Tucson Estates major shareholder is none other than the president's only son."

Shit! I thought. How did shithead get hold of that kind of money? I half knew the answer to that one already. Real estate in NYC has traditionally been the means through which Italian Organized Crime, what the F.B.I. routinely refers to, in its internal documentation, as I.O.C., launders vast sums of money.

"This is where it gets interesting," Slater continued, "Recently Tucson Estates was the beneficiary of an undisclosed loan that enabled it to meet its obligations. Its obligations totaled nine hundred million dollars."

Coughing up almost a billion when all your assets are in the red, is no mean feat.

"Who put up the money then?" I asked.

"Alberto Motisi," Slater said. "The same person you're supposed to deliver the data to."

Context. It changes everything.

"You knew all this?"

"I knew some of it. Not the amount of money involved, nor who had fronted it. Tucson Estates are a client of mine."

"You piece of shit!"

"Alex, I didn't know. They don't confide everything in me. It's only afterwards I found out. The president's son told me some, right before he disappeared. The rest I had to dig out. Piece together myself."

"When were you going to tell me?"

"I couldn't get hold of you," he reminded me.

For those who've never heard of him, Alberto Motisi was the unindicted, unacknowledged head of the The Sacra Corona Unita (SCU), or United Sacred Crown.

It's a shadowy, mafia criminal organization from the region of Apulia in Italy that's involved in political corruption cases, gun running, influence peddling and the ever ubiquitous drugs that go with all of this.

It's made alliances with international criminal organizations such as the Russian and Albanian mafias, the Colombian drug cartels, and some Asian organizations. And never has a single New York State prosecutor ever managed to get as much as a shred of verifiable evidence that could stand up in a court of law.

In the world of Italian Organized Crime the United Scared Crown is a will of the wisp. And its head was my destination.

Tonight.

"You still have the data?" Slater asked again.

I should have realized of course. I would have had I been paying attention. But questions of betrayal. My memories of what Wendy had done. What I had done in return occupied half of my mind.

Slater's betrayal, such as it was, was easier to understand. And Alberto Motisi was now, I thought, the person to whom I owed my life to.

"At some point twenty thousand dollars stop having a lot of value," I said.

"You still have it? We can renegotiate."

"I have it I said," and I knew I'd made a mistake the moment the words left my lips. I tried, in vain, to correct it. To claw back the words. To explain things further so that I wouldn't be so exposed. I made a gesture with my right hand, my mind racing on how to cover up. My body shifted ever so slightly.

There's no such thing as an average sniper rifle bullet. Each sniper has his favorite, plus there are dictates that arise out of circumstances. What access he has to long guns in a civilian setting. Where he can place them. How far he expects to be able to shoot.

A .30-06 Springfield, for instance, has an effective range of just over a thousand yards and its 165g cartridge travels at two thousand end eight hundred feet per second.

At that speed it reaches its target before the noise of the rifle or the sonic boom of the bullet. When I was young I read Erich Maria Remarque's anti-war novel *All Quiet On The Western Front*. I remembered how he mentioned that you never hear the sound of the shot that kills you.

I felt a tag on my left shoulder. The irony of words and moments. Had I not moved at that precise moment as I'd tried to claw back my words and explain to Slater it would have been my head.

The bullet an inch or so below the top of the shoulder, pierced the fleshy part of it, exited just below the clavicle without touching the bone. Jerked me forward as if I'd been pushed from behind.

"Ugh," I went. Incredulously. Brain vainly trying to compute sensations it'd never experienced before. The cavitation effect caused by 7.62x63mm round travelling at nearly three thousand feet per second numbed my entire shoulder. Paralyzed my left arm. Caused my heart to miss a beat so that it felt like it caught. A momentary heavy weight, deep inside my chest.

The round then exited in a spray of bright red blood. The spatter blossoming on Slater's crisp white shirt worn so he would be visible to someone looking through a scope from a distance. And entered his chest.

Slater made a soft gurgling sound. He was virtually lifted off his feet by the force of the slowing round. He fell back on his back feet kicking wildly. The front of his white shirt now dyed a deep, persistent red that in the poor light of the park looked glistening black.

Self-preservation took over almost immediately. My guess is also that my dark, non-reflective clothing made me that much harder to hit from a distance.

Pressing a hand into my injured shoulder, feeling the warm seep of blood between my fingers, I crouched low and moved as fast as I could. From somewhere in the darkness in front of me I heard the familiar cough of the semi-automatic weapons my two escorts carried. Saw a single muzzle flash light up the night again and again.

"This way," Tomas was by my side. Helping me steady myself. Guiding me. "Keep your head down," he said needlessly. Michal's weapon kept coughing again and again. "He's on that tall building, behind us," Tomas pointed with his weapon, clutched still in one hand.

I tried to look but the numbness in my left shoulder made it difficult to turn my head. Out of the corner of my eye I saw the lines of a tall building overlooking the park, outlined against the night sky.

A boom sounded from somewhere above us and Michal's weapon coughed back in response. Another boom. This time the bullet hit the ground not half an inch from where I was.

"Shit! Move!" Tomas tugged me harder. With his free hand he raised his weapon and let off a series of coughs aimed at where he thought the sniper was. "Let's get you to the car," I could hear concern deep in his voice.

Boom. This time there was no reply back from Michal.

"Quickly," Tomas was practically dragging me. We got to the car and opened the doors. The boom sounded again this time. He seemed to trip towards the car. Put out his arm holding the gun to steady himself. The weapon struck the driver side window and the top part of the roof. Fell from his nerveless fingers with a metal clatter. His other hand released its grip of me. And he was dead.

***

111

Humans don't have many instincts. Our frontal lobes take over so much of our activity that it becomes difficult to ascertain what is conscious thought and what isn't. But that doesn't mean we don't have any instincts and running away from danger is one of them.

I was hurt. And in danger. And though I was willing, at any point up to now, to put my life in harm's way and feel it end. Having taken a bullet that damaged me, dying was the furthest thing from my mind.

Doubled up. Hand pressed hard against the wound in my shoulder, I slang away through the night, making still in the general direction of the Hudson Yards.

Fate, it seems, is a mistress that not only likes to play cruel games but loves to, on top of everything else, rub salt in deep wounds.

***

I was fairly sure I was dying. I didn't feel like I was. The lack of that sensation actually was what convinced me that I was dying. The human body has so many nerves and capillaries, arteries and veins that a bullet that pretty much numbs your entire left side and paralyzes your arm is sure to have caused some major damage.

The lack of pain was convincing me that the damage was severe enough for my body to no longer need to signal pain. It was experiencing what could only be catastrophic events that were beginning to end it.

Not far behind me I could hear police sirens. Again. It'd been a busy day for the cops today and most of it was down to me. Or, rather it was down to those who were trying to get to me.

I was in Central Park at night. I had entered on the Madison Avenue side. Traversed it cleaving to the 97th St Transverse and was near the far edge on the Central Park West side.

112

How long did I have, exactly?

Not sure.

The blood flow from my wound had slowed down considerably thanks to the pressure I was applying and my shoulder was beginning to throb. A deep, dull ache that seemed to be timed with my heartbeats. From a distance however, in the dark, I was just another homeless drunk lying on a bench.

In my frantic attempts to run I'd lost my earpiece so I had to get my phone from my pocket to contact my Watcher.

"You still alive?"

"How many dead?"

"Three. Slater. Two other men."

"You know where I am going."

"You OK?"

"No. I need help. Can you contact Motisi?"

"What? No way! You crazy?"

"I have no other choice. I need help and his men are dead. The ones he sent to make sure I would reach him."

"Motisi is not what I would call cooperative,"

Who, ever has a choice?

"I will quadruple your fee."

"Twenty thousand?"

"Yep."

"Hang on." The connection went dead.

I let my head rest back against the hardness of the wood. My plan was to get patched up and cleave all the way to Central Park West from inside the park, emerging at Columbus Circle so I could head for Hudson Yards.

My phone vibrated. I picked up. "Yo," my Watcher's comforting voice.

"Do we have an agreement?"

"We do. Hang on."

"Do you know where I am?"

"I've triangulated you. Hang on."

"Thank you." I said and for once the words were more than a convention. I was suddenly grateful to a human being I had never met before and was unlikely to ever meet. Ever.

17 – Assistance

An injured body is a malfunctioning machine. I wasn't sure how much blood I'd lost but it was enough to make me feel dizzy and weak. I lay back on the bench and felt the tendrils of darkness wrap themselves around my consciousness.

Darkness is so seductive. It erases everything you are. It rubs out your cares. It takes away your pain. You abandon yourself to it and as it dissolves you, it absolves you.

Absolution is lack of care. You no longer worry about what you did, what you didn't do, about what you are about to do.

I was no innocent.

In my mind's cry I confessed. Kill me. I said. I deserve it.

***

"Alex?" The voice brought me back. I felt groggy. Eyes swollen shut. "Alex, wake up."

I was dreaming. I blinked but in the darkness I could barely see the outline of the man, boy? Teen in front of me.

"You?" I croaked.

"There's no one else right now Alex. This shit's real." I tried to close my eyes. Sink back into the abyss and a hand slapped me.

The sound was like a thunderclap in my ears. The sensation sent sparks across my vision. No. I screamed but no sound came out. Let me be. Another slap. One more.

"What's your name?" I asked. My voice slurred.

"No names,"

"Com'on. You owe me that at least."

"Leroy," the voice that should be on the phone said.

"Why are you here?"

"There's no one else Alex. Motisi cannot mobilize men quickly enough. The city is in virtual lockdown."

"Lockdown?"

"Homeland Security are pulling some kind of stunt. Until it gets cleared up his men are constrained."

"Homeland?"

"Yeah. Heavy shit. For now, it's just me. I'm all you got. Good thing we've hit it off from the start, hey?"

I smiled. Then winced as he did something to my shoulder. I felt a tug. Then pain. Then nothing much at all. Then more tugs.

"The wound looks clean. No broken bones and the bleeding's almost stopped. Talk about being super lucky."

"Yeah, super lucky. I repeated. Only got shot once."

"Don't be a wise guy. Sniper bullets are no joke. This one went clean through. Missed major arteries and didn't hit any bones. I've cleaned it for you. Applied an anesthetic for the pain."

"You a doctor as well?"

"Third year medical student."

"Aah, I see."

"Take this. In case there is an infection." He gave me some pills. "One every four hours until they run out."

I put them in my pocket.

"Can you sit up?"

I did. The ground swam in front of my eyes.

"Dizzy, right?"

"A little."

"Not sure how much blood you've lost. Your Tee's pretty soaked though." As he talked he placed a rubber tourniquet above my elbow. There was the burning sensation of a needle. Then, he was holding some kind of IV drip. A clear plastic bag which he squeezed to pump it in me. "Saline solution," he explained. "It'll bring your volume pressure back up."

He worked a little more on my shoulder. Gave me one more pill to swallow. I stopped asking questions.

Eventually I sat up. He expertly removed the needle from the inside of my elbow and placed a band aid over the tiny wound it'd left behind.

"Feeling better?"

"Yes, thank you Leroy,"

"You're paying for all this." He said. "Here," he offered me something I couldn't quite see.

"More pills?"

"Car keys. You're in no shape to walk any more."

"What's going on?"

"Lots of chatter. I need to get back otherwise you will be truly blind. Bottom line, government wants you dead. Don't die before you pay the balance of what you owe us."

Before I could say anything else he disappeared into the night.

Of all the things that'd happened to me tonight Leroy was easily the most surreal. I began to wonder just how deep the Watchers went and who were they really. How had he got to me so fast?

I touched my hand to my shoulder. There was heavy binding there. Everything held tightly together with heavy duty surgical tape. I felt no pain but the stiffness was still there. I had some mobility back in that arm, which was good. At least, I thought, I wasn't dying.

I exited Central Park at the height of the New York Historical Society building. The car keys had a label on them: "West 76th Street & Columbus Avenue" it read. I pressed the key and a Ford Focus beep and flashed its lights at me.

Small and NYC streets friendly. Plus it was an easy car to drive for someone like me. How had Leroy managed all this? Inside the car, between the driver and passenger seat was ab earpiece. I took it, checked to see it was charged. Placed it in my ear. With my phone I dialed.

"Yo,"

"The car?"

"I'd like to take all the credit but Motisi did that. And the drugs. I just had to deliver them."

"Ok. I will keep this channel open for now." I said.

"Sure,"

I turned on the engine. Eased the car out of parking and joined the flow of evening traffic on Columbus Avenue. The Hudson Yards were not that far away.

18 – Certainty

If quantum gravity were ever solved cause and effect could be reversed. The events themselves existing as a purely speculative state where, exactly like Schrodinger's cat, cause an defect could be superimposed upon each other. One being the cause or the effect of the other.

When we are caught up in the moment we can only react. We pay the bills because they arrive. We choose from the menu because the waiter is there. We say "I love you" because someone says it to us first. We run because something scared us.

The point is that though we appear to choose to perform all these actions they are actually foisted on us by expectations, circumstances, evolution and (maybe) tradition. None of them are truly intentional. Otherwise we'd arrange to pay bills in advance (because we know they're coming), our choice of menu would have been made long before the waiter came and hovered over us, we'd say "I love you" proactively and when something scares us we'd choose to stand our ground and fight.

These are actions that require way more effort than reactions. They require intent. And intent suggests planning. Planning leads us to a future. A future has hope in it, built-in.

Wendy's actions hurt me. You could say I responded to that hurt. But what if my own actions were completely intentional?

What if, everything I did had a predetermined outcome I could see, a potential I could gauge and yet I still went ahead and did it anyway?

You can see how tricky this stuff gets once you start to think about it. And that's with cause and effect being linear. There is no quantum gravity theory to grapple with just yet. Or rather, yes; the theory exists but in a very raw, rudimentary stage at the moment. It can be ignored.

What cannot be ignored is the current, indisputable, irreversible chain of cause and effect. The streets outside unfolded like in the movies. The city that never sleeps never fails to live up to its name. It also, sadly, presents a façade made of smokes and mirrors, naked greed and raw need, personal dreams and innocent hope.

The superlatives fail to do it justice. New York City streets energize me and depress me in equal measure. And, as I rolled into the Hudson Yards with the iconic lattice work structure and the towering buildings, I could only think of how the city had an energy that consumed its inhabitants, fired them up and burnt them out.

I could, quite happily that night, decouple cause and effect. Make the night never start. Some events never happen. Some lives that were lost, come back.

Wendy would have liked that.

I was at the Hudson Yards because I needed a laptop to work with. I needed one here because in the entire city I now had no one I could really trust.

"You there?" I touched the earpiece to bring it to life.

"Yo, Alex. I am listening."

"Anything new?"

"At the moment no one quite knows where you are. But that's not going to last long. Everyone's out looking for you."

Yeah, I thought. Great, and filed that new piece of metadata away.

"Alex, listen," he paused for a second presaging what was coming. "It's getting a little uncomfortable this end." He said. "There are some serious players with capabilities we cannot fend off forever. Helping you always leaves a trace."

"Are they closing in on you?" I asked.

"Not just yet. You're too high priority for everyone right now. But inevitably they will find us."

"How long can you give me."

"Half an hour?"

I digested that.

"Alex I'm sorry. If you want to renegotiate the price."

"No, we're good. You came out yourself." I reeled off a number for him, a password and an authorization code. "There's twenty five thousand in that account. Leave the five. Just in case I make it."

"Alex-"

"Do one more thing for me," I cut him off. Nothing quite spells out finality than openly sharing bank account logins and passwords.

"What?"

"Patch me through to this number." I reeled it off for him.

"Ok."

"In case I have to go dark without warning. Alex, I'm sorry."

"Sure," he kept apologizing when really it should be the other way around. Everything is a system. The system follows its own internal rules. Its integrity relies upon blind obedience to those rules with totally expected outcomes. This is why I walk instead of take a car on data runs. Usually.

Walking introduces random factors. Cars, trains, airplanes, they may as well be on grooves with a fixed starting point and a predetermined ending one.

Systems hate inconsistency. Uncertainty kills them.

"Hello," the voice at the other end of the connection wasn't familiar. It'd been some time before I heard it, but I relied on my being correct.

Human behavior is also a system. We're hardwired to connect. The social component in us underpins so many of our processes that to suppress it or ignore it only invites trouble. Recluses are damaged people.

Sociability requires reciprocation because that's how you get empathy and empathy is an emotion we use to understand the motives of those we don't yet know and predict their behavior sufficiently well to trust them.

Reciprocation calls for the return of a favor. Every system, in some way, runs on favors.

It'd been a strange data run. One where a particular design of a particular chemical formula had to get to its destination from NYC to Bahrain where a specific lab would carry out experiments for a private manufacturer of psychoactive chemicals.

There were complications. There's no such thing as walking from NYC to Bahrain. You have to trust in guided, predetermined systems. Introduce randomness in other ways. In its execution I'd gained a favor. One I was now calling in.

"Dr Bergrow?" I asked.

"Who is this?"

"It's Alex." I expected instant recognition. I was disappointed.

"Alex who?" The job had been three years ago. When I was still starting out. When Wendy and I thought the world would have a place for both of us.

"Just Alex,"

Long pause. Then: "Oh,"

"I need something from you," I said.

***

Was it coincidence that he was in the Hudson Yards? Real estate is hard to come by in NYC. Harder still in Manhattan. At some point, as availability runs out physics takes over. There is only so much available space in this particular location. Only so many people can be accommodated. This

122

makes it inevitable that some data points will rub against some other ones and locations will then become predetermined.

Infinite potential is a theoretical pipedream. Everyone is constrained in some way. Behavior then comes down to a handful of variables at the most. Everything is predetermined, to a degree. The zip code for Hudson Yards is 10001. The address I needed to get to, afterwards, was just a skip and a jump away. Draw your own conclusions about fate.

I passed, on the way, Yotel New York.

I'd tracked Wendy's phone there. Her laptop. Called in reception with a description for a delivery. Got confirmation of the room number.

Systems.

I'd called the dispatcher. Distressed voice. Saw a man with a gun. Gave the address. Room number. Everyone's scared of mass shootings. Fear feeds into perception. Perception changes reality. Action then takes place according to what is perceived instead of what is.

Simples.

I was hurt. Angry.

I watched on the news as the SWAT team swarmed in. Cordoned off the outside. Dispatched a team to go inside.

What happened next plays like a movie file stored in a hidden internal drive of my mind.

The door to the room swings open. The manager, mindful of the cost, uses a master keycard. There is a cannister. Smoke. Screams. SWAT team go in. Standard two by two formation.

Gas masks. All in black. Knees bent to provide stability. Heckler & Koch MP5s at the ready. Red beams from the guns' laser sights crisscrossing the smoke as they dissect the room. Voices. Screams. Confusion.

A man and a woman. On the bed.

"Don't move!"

"Show us your hands!"

Standard commands. It should end there.

The woman is smart however. Realizes what's going on. She's angry. Knowledge is a bug. It makes predetermined events in a system behave in a randomized fashion. Knowledge changes behavior because it introduces certainty in situations where uncertainty is the norm.

Paradoxically, it makes the outcome less, not more predictable. Knowledge risks changing projected behavior. The outcome becomes unpredictable.

I thought Wendy and her lover would be taken in for questioning. Her lies to me exposed as I'd have to come and bail her out, maybe. That bit part of my expectations is a bit hazy because I too did not think that far ahead.

Pain. Reaction.

My actions were a reaction.

Wendy understood. She was angry. Adrenaline in the bloodstream shuts down some functions. Allows others. Did she think before she reached for her phone by the bed?

Was it a movement driven purely by anger?

Was there a factoring of possibilities on her part?

These are questions that will never be answered.

A view through a Heckler & Koch MP5 aperture sight produces a metal circle with a tiny, raised, metal line at its nadir. Viewed through the glass of a gas mask, in a room where there is still some swirling smoke it becomes a tunnel through which vision travels. The vision guides the mind in a single-minded, task-specific action.

This is the sight of a gun. The gun has a trigger. Sight, gun and trigger are a system too. The muzzle velocity of a bullet fired by this weapon is one thousand, three hundred and ninety four feet per second. Set on semi-automatic fire there was time perhaps for just two bullets to leave the system. Messengers of death.

They caught Wendy in mid-action. The phone already in her hand. They stopped her from completing the motion. Flung her body back. The sheet she held with one hand to her chest to cover up her nakedness blossomed crimson. Her body, flailing back in cinematic slow motion. Phone going flying from her dead hand to land on the floor beside the bed. Its screen starred by the impact with the floor.

In the time it took for it to hit the ground vulnerable arteries had ruptured. Massive systemic shock had caused the heart to spasm, miss beats. Suffer damage.

Meanwhile the projectiles emitted by the weapon had done their job. Message delivered.

***

The last piece of the puzzle. The thing everybody was willing to kill or die for. Dr Bergrow was incidental here. A background fixture that happened to be useful same way as a handle on a door is useful.

I was short on time and high on the pills Leroy had given me. I checked to see if he was still there but there was no response to my call.

He'd gone dark. Or worse.

I could almost feel the net closing in around me. Panic setting in because of my inability to suddenly see. Without a Watcher I was vulnerable. Just another stiff in the street. A lab rat in a system that watched everything.

Dr Bergrow met me at the bottom of latticework building. He was visibly agitated even at a distance.

"Alex?" his voice was tight with tension. He became even more agitated as he took in the dark stains on my Tee. The bandages on my left shoulder and my disheveled appearance.

"Dr Bergrow," I said.

"I can only give you a few minutes. Then we're done here."

It sounded ungrateful, but I understood. I took the laptop he had with him. Connected it to my phone.

It took a few minutes to decrypt everything. I looked at the exact same satellite images I'd seen only hours ago with the same degree of ignorance.

Context. Context changes data. Nine hundred million dollars worth of information was staring me in the face. There were coordinates where the pictures were taken. Names. Dates. A time-stamp.

This is why you need to see the data. It's not just what it is. It's what it signifies. The metadata is an additional, higher-level layer of data. There is metadata on top of that. Context provides meaning.

Back home. In my apartment I had the TV set on all the time. It's background noise. I know my brain picks up all sorts of things. The always-on news cycle makes me feel I am connected to the world.

Titbits stick to mind. Things that are current but have no meaning because there is nothing to hang them on. Nothing that will transform them from data to information.

A raid. Some mansion on the Hamptons. A financier I'd never heard of running an underaged sex scheme. He was connected. Scientists. Government personnel.

I looked at the decrypted satellite imagery.

"Give me your phone," I said to Dr Bergrow.

"Will this take long?"

"Almost done. Then we're even."

He passed it to me. I used his data to look up coordinates for the Hamptons. Handed it back to him.

The rest was guesswork. Government vehicles have unique signifiers. Digital signals that are tracked in case of attack or kidnapping. I didn't have to delve too deeply in all this. If the mansion on the pictures was the financiers and of that I was pretty sure it was, then the imagery showed government personnel visiting it, in person, on specific times and days.

Data is a smoking gun.

It can put you in a place where you'd rather never be found in.

How had shithead got hold of this? Still, I could see why it was worth what it was.

Systems.

"Thanks," I said to the Doc. I handed him back his laptop. Phone. He took them without a word. Watched me as I ambled away, heading towards the part of the Yards that was under construction. All shadows and machinery.

He was already outside my thoughts. I considered what I knew. What I'd found out.

Every system is fragile. Its working parameters come with a tipping point. Push it beyond the tipping point and the system will crash. No matter how robust it may seem to be. A human heart is designed to beat maybe two billion times give or take a few million. Temporarily overload its capacity however and it goes into systemic shock. Tears itself apart.

"Don't move!"

Shit. Without a Watcher I was a sitting duck. Blind. Helpless. One good thing. If the person that'd told me not to move wanted me dead, I'd be dead already, I thought. That meant I had a chance.

"Don't shoot," I said. And moving slowly, without turning around I put both hands up.

***

There comes a moment in a man's life when everything that was before has to balance with everything that is yet to come. Some people call this Karma, others will tell you it's a form of Zen. For me it is simply Now.

Of course, intellectually and even philosophically elegant as this may sound, there are some details which once taken into account will make you change your mind.

Like the fact that I'm on my knees, with my hands behind my head, staring at the shadowy form of a man holding a snub nosed .38 and pointing it directly at the forehead of Alex Logan Esquire, a.k.a. yours truly, from no less than a foot away.

It's not a great situation to be in, especially when you're negotiating which is, actually, exactly what I was doing at that moment in time. Granted, it's difficult to see the leverage I possessed but that will become evident in a moment, along with the curious journey that took to that seminal moment in my life where, like Schrodinger's famous cat I was in stasis: neither dead nor alive until the finger that was pressing on the trigger of the gun, reached the 10lbs of pressure required to trip the hammer and fire a 125 grain bullet at a speed of upwards of 770 feet per second, directly into my brain.

I know that this is not quite what Schrodinger envisioned as the collapse of his probability wave but I am willing to wager that it's a pretty cool way to visualize his, admittedly difficult to understand, thought experiment.

The .30 Special pointing at my forehead, in this particular case, is the measuring device that will determine whether I am dead or alive. Its moment of measurement represented by the pull of a trigger and the fall of a hammer on a primer embedded in a metal cased cartridge. Kneeling there, hands behind my head, forehead an easy target, I am visualizing the entire process in a deconstructionist way that strips back the layers of time and creates, for me, the perfect way to relieve the pressure of the moment and think clearly.

I know you think that is odd. Let me assure you this won't be the first time you will think this though, quite possibly, there is a more than slim possibility that it will be the last.

Bear with me.

The man's face is a mystery to me. Hidden by the shadows cast by the powerful lights behind him. I know his name: Ned. Though that may be a decoy.

At times like this a respectable, law-abiding citizen has several options. Option One: give up. Give the man with the gun exactly what he wants. It may work or it may not, but you can understand why most people don't take the time to factor in the possibilities. Presented with a gun with a barrel pointed directly at you, they tend to fold. Do as the man with the gun says and hope for the best.

I don't fall within the normal distribution of your statistical Bell Curve. I am a little perverse that way.

Option Two: Plead for clemency and hope for mercy. It takes little insight to realize that the chances of your average respectable, law-abiding citizen finding themselves at the docs, past midnight, on their knees, with a gun pointed at their heads are pretty slim. This means that I am neither respectable nor law-abiding, though both of these characterizations are up for debate.

Seeing how both respectability and obedience to the laws that run a particular society are a matter of perception and interpretation the correct answer to either question relies on interpretation. To my eyes I am both respectable and, within context, law-abiding. But that is a purely semantic approach that takes into account the network effect of linked behaviors.

I am sure the man with the gun will disagree which is what makes this situation particularly sticky. Depending on interpretation he may be, even when his current action is taken into account, more law-abiding than I.

Which leads me to Option Three: Determine the weight of the factors that lead to the trigger being pulled and the gun being fired against the weight of the factors that call for the exact opposite.

This is not so hard to imagine. Consider that if I (or you) happened to be Schrodinger's cat, in order to survive we would have to arrest the collapse of the probability wave and remain in stasis forever. Neither dead, nor alive is much more preferable to being definitely dead. Avoiding the certainty of the first of the probabilities increases the likelihood of returning to the warm embrace of the second.

All we'd have to do, in our virtual cat state, to achieve that option is find a plausible way to influence the willingness of the person with the measuring apparatus to carry out the measurement.

You see what I've done here. I know the man with the gun wants, somewhere deep in him, to press the trigger and erase the narrative of my existence forever. But he is not operating in a vacuum. His presence here has been dictated by other forces and other events which, when linked correctly, weave a web of interactions and connections that lead to a degree of accountability.

His actions, in other words, are not free of consequences.

A smart cat, like you and I, just needs a means of bringing those consequences to the present so that they can command his attention and stay the increasing pressure being applied by his finger on the trigger.

And we'd have to do this quickly enough. With sufficient aplomb to avoid triggering the idea that what we have here is a modified version of Option Two which is most likely to trigger him (pun unintended).

It's a predicament. Especially when Option One, which is what he really wants us to go for before he pulls that trigger, is never really on the cards. Never will be.

Tricky.

"Mr Motisi will be angry with you," I say. He's taken me to a part of the site where there are hardly any lights. There is no suppressor to his gun but a snub nosed .30 Special isn't a particularly noisy weapon.

"Lots of people want you dead Alex," he says.

"I know," no point in denying it. My guess is he's a cop. NYPD detective. There is an NYPD Tow Pound not far from where we are. Was he stationed there? Visiting? His finding me is that undefined variable that happens when the wrong people get to be in the right place or vice versa because there is no opportunity to see the data from afar. Perceive the pattern. Understand it. Take action.

Without a Watcher I was blind.

"I could shoot you right now," he says.

"True. You could. But then a billion dollar investment would fizz away. Evaporate."

"What you're talking about?"

"Mr Motisi paid that much for what is inside the head you're pointing a gun at," I said.

He wavered. I could almost see the calculations in his head. Play the mob card. Get some favor. Money. But it's the mob. Play the cop card. Be a hero. Earn some respect. But you can't eat respect and being a hero doesn't provide for your future.

Choices. Consequences.

The secret to successful negotiating is to know going in that you aren't going to win every point. Decide in advance what parts are important and what parts you're willing to concede. And never, ever concede beyond your "walk-away" point.

I wasn't going to be let go here. That much was clear.

A problem doesn't go away by ignoring it.

So I presented solutions. "I have information people have died for tonight," I said.

"So, you're the one that's caused all this?"

"No. I didn't cause anything Ned. May I call you Ned?" I can see his head nod. "the president's son caused that when he got hold of some top secret information."

"Like hell he did,"

"Hear me out. The case in The Hamptons, the pedophile ring. That goes deeper than you might even think."

"That's bullshit," I can almost see his finger tightening on the trigger.

"No. It's not." I am careful to modulate my voice. Not feed into his fear. Behavior is contagious. I am calm and under control. I call the shots here. Not him. "There are satellite networks," I paint a very broad picture for him. "They take pictures. Even when they're not supposed to. Everything they photograph is logged." I could almost visualize some data analyst somewhere tagging the picture files from the satellite system overhead and putting it in the system.

"Satellites that are not designed to spy on U.S. citizens, actually do so." That, was only part of the scandal. The perfect storm happens when a lot of unlikely elements come together. And each feeds into the other. "There are powerful people in our government who are as human as you and I. Power likes getting away with things. It likes indulging from time to time. It likes to feel that it is above you and me."

I could see I was getting through to him. First the cop. Then the person.

"Some powerful people couldn't resist but give in to the urge to feed that itch for getting away with things. They visited a certain financier's mansion in The Hamptons. Tasted the forbidden fruit. Unfortunately for them the financier stopped being able to outrun public opinion. The growing number of victims from his past willing to openly speak out against him. These things accumulate."

Of course power is power. The connections and evidence tenuous. Almost.

"But they can thankfully deny everything. Put out press releases stating their own shock. Expressing their outrage. How they'd been duped. But we have eyes everywhere. Data flows through this amazing system of ours. And an eye in the sky had seen some of them. Identified them. Placing them directly where they shouldn't be at a time when they publicly stated they couldn't have been."

He understood what I was saying.

"That's a scandal no system can contain. You and I can't do much with this information. We're too small. We can be made to go away. But Mr Motisi however …"

I left my sentence unfinished on purpose. The golden rule of negotiating: let the other party work to fill-in the blanks for you. Let them become invested in the common outcome you're working for.

"He will reward you handsomely," I added finally. "And he's not far from here."

He stepped then into a feeble ray of light. He's maybe forty-five. Slightly balding. And very pale looking, like he only comes out at night.

Vice then? I didn't know.

"If you lied to me – " he said at last.

"I haven't," conveniently I left out the part of the decrypted data. The one where he could just shoot me, take my phone and peddle the data himself for enough money to buy a small planet.

That bit of information was not one that would lead me to the outcome I wanted.

"Come with me," he leans in and puts a hand on my Tee and hauls me to my feet. I try not to wince at the pain I am feeling in my shoulder. "This way," he points me towards the water's edge in the distance.

19 – Delivery

Tribeca 10007 had a doorman. Of course. A uniformed guy at reception. But I was with a cop.

"Apartment 409. We're here for Alberto," the cop says. The doorman looks suspiciously at me but the badge is real. He waves us in.

What happened next is an anti-climax. Tension is generated by a desire to survive against the odds. To come out alive. I no longer had that desire. I was perfectly, serenely, reconciled with my fate.

Goons at the door outside the apartment. Goons inside. Burly men with guns. They pat down me and cop. Take my phone. His. His gun. Show us in.

Alberto Motisi is younger than I'd expected. Slim. Black haired. Clean shaven.

"Do you need a doctor?" His concern appears genuine. I shrug.

"I am sorry for your men," I say. He nods.

The cop then has his turn. A question about money. A bag is brought. Cash. A lot of cash. A favor too. He blanches in that he cannot believe it is so easy.

I wonder if his body will be found floating in the water before the night is out. But maybe Motisi doesn't operate quite like that.

"You can go now," he tells the cop. "Do you need a ride back? One of my man- "

"No, I'm good." He's holding the bag. His face a mix of emotions warring with each other.

I watch him being escorted out.

"You want to sit?" I am invited to and I slump in a chair. I am conscious of the fact that my clothes are stained with blood. Both my own and that of others. What a crazy night it's been.

"You have what I want?" Alberto finally asks. Straight to the point.

"I do. What are you going to do with it?"

"What a strange question Mr Logan. Why should you care?"

I wouldn't. Normally, I wouldn't. This is different. I try to explain. I am not sure how far I get.

Leverage. Power. Untouchability. I explain about two worlds. One in the light and one in the shadows. How the world of the light holds itself up to be righteous. Anointed by nature almost to receive every benefit of the system. While the world of the shadows is a bad one. An evil one. To be tolerated. Used. Discarded. Hunted down even.

Then I said how these two are reversed. How the ones in the light have shadows they hide in and do what they hunt the ones in the shadows for. It's not right. At some point, someone must make a stand.

I stop.

Alberto is in his seat. An expensive whiskey tumbler in one hand. He has offered me one already and I've declined. I am in no shape to contain alcohol.

"Interesting take," he says at last. I have no idea what he's thinking. "If you could choose Mr Logan, what would you have me do?"

"Release the information," I said. "Shine a very bright light on the dark underbelly of the system."

"But wouldn't that make it burn?" he asks.

"Yes, it would. Burn them." I say, "Burn them all."

And I'm spent. Uncaring now what happens to me next. My stupidity had killed Wendy, I thought. But it was the system that had actually killed her. The perfect weapon. With me, the trigger.

None of us can ever be happy in such a world because none of us deserve to.

"There is a question about your money," he said. I was about to say that it no longer mattered but he finished the sentence before I could speak. "Already wired into your account. I, too, am sorry about your friend."

"Slater wasn't really my friend," I said.

"No, I mean, the young men. The medical student?"

I frown.

"A routine traffic light stop gone wrong, as so many seem to these days." He says. "He was mistakenly shot dead. There will be an investigation, of course, I understand but the evidence will show probable cause. The officers acting lawfully."

I feel outrage. I don't show it.

"What are you going to do?" I ask. "With the data?"

"I will think about it."

His goons show me to the door. I take the elevator ride to the ground floor alone.

Alone.

I am none.

And this has been so bad I am fully prepared to die.

20 – Chaos

News: riots. Crowds waving placards in NYC streets. People demanding justice.

The 24-hour news cycle is full of revelations. Information linking some of the most respected names in the worlds of science, business and government to tales of underaged sex, the trafficking of young women. All-night parties fueled by booze and drugs.

The Hamptons as a den of inequity. Whitewashed veneer hiding the worst vices.

I barely notice any more.

Each day brings something new. Someone caves in and talks. Someone breaks and makes a deal.

There is an unending roster of prominent people whose transgressions go back decades.

It's like watching the Nuremberg Trials through the lens of Reality TV. Not so young women recall when they were first groomed for the life. There are apologists. Explainers. People who are denying they'd even known anything.

No one's buying it.

The system is tearing itself apart. So it should.

I am not data running anymore.

What am I going to do with my life?

I don't know.

I will think of something some time soon.

www.ingramcontent.com/pod-product-compliance
Lightning Source LLC
Chambersburg PA
CBHW060940050726
47592CB00003B/1034